D1708104

Pandora's Box

Beginning's End

Lisa L. Stevenson

iUniverse, Inc.
New York Bloomington

Pandora's Box
Beginning's End

iUniverse books may be ordered through booksellers or by contacting:

iUniverse
1663 Liberty Drive
Bloomington, IN 47403
www.iuniverse.com
1-800-Authors (1-800-288-4677)

ISBN: 978-0-595-48097-5 (pbk)
ISBN: 978-0-595-71620-3 (cloth)
ISBN: 978-0-595-60196-7 (ebk)

Printed in the United States of America

iUniverse rev. date: 2/6/2009

Prologue

Life is full of choices, some hard, some not so hard; others are downright impossible. Some are even life-altering. Everyone has that one moment—that defining moment that sets him on his path, that moment when all that he is comes face to face with all that he can be. It is the choice that he makes at that moment that shapes who he will become … and this was Jeremy's.

Jeremy paused outside the door as he collected his thoughts. What was the going price for his soul again? Oh, yeah, a seat in the Senate. He knocked.

A pretty young woman opened the door. "Hello, Jeremy." She motioned him inside. "He's waiting for you in the den."

"Do you know what he wants?"

"I suppose he'll tell you that when he sees you." The woman pulled on her coat.

"Where are you going?"

"Don't worry, Jeremy. You'll do just fine. I suspect you're more like the old man than you think." She smiled reassuringly as she closed the door behind her.

"Are you in, or are you out? Make a decision," the elderly man called from the other room.

Jeremy steadied his nerves and reluctantly entered the room.

"That's it, Jeremy. I knew you could do it." He smiled and extended his hand to Jeremy.

Jeremy forced the corners of his lips upward as he shook the man's hand. It was cold and moist, just as he had remembered. He wanted to recoil in disgust. He felt the hairs on the back of his neck tingle.

"Cold hands, huh?" the man teased.

Even colder heart, Jeremy thought as he gratefully reclaimed his hand. He had to fight the urge to wipe his hand on his pants leg. "So why am I here?"

"Right to business, huh? I like that in an employee." The man eased himself into the overstuffed recliner. "It's time for you to start earning my millions in contributions. I'd like a drink. You want a drink?"

"Yes, sir, I could use one right about now."

"Fix me a bourbon, and while you're at it, fix one for yourself."

As Jeremy poured the two drinks, he felt the old man's eyes boring into him. Suddenly, he felt something else. Something grabbed the cuff of his pants. "What the—?" Jeremy dropped the glass as he spun around and grabbed for the edge of the bar to steady himself.

The elderly man smiled triumphantly.

Jeremy forced himself to look under the bar. His mind kept denying what his eyes were seeing. It was a young boy, badly beaten and curled into the fetal position.

"Anything wrong?" the man asked.

"How ... old is that child?" Jeremy's mind was reeling. He wished he could just go back to before he knocked on that door. "Who is he? Where did he come from?"

"He's nine; his name is Gregory, and I picked him up at the park. Any more questions before we get back to business?"

"That's the child from the headlines. What in hell is he doing here?"

"'In hell'? That's a pretty good description. I suppose he *is* in hell right now." The man laughed. "He's my new recruit, and I like to spend one-on-one time with all my children when they first arrive. Initial imprinting is so important you know? I think he'll make a fine soldier. Don't you?"

"For your own army?"

"No. It won't be my army."

"Are you crazy? Do you know what they'll do to us—to me—if they find us here with this boy? It won't matter whether or not I helped you steal him. Just knowing he's here is enough to land me in prison for the rest of my life."

"Then we better get started, so you can hurry and get out of here." The man tossed Jeremy an envelope.

Jeremy just looked at the envelope, and then turned his attentions back to the boy. The man was old and feeble. He was sure he could save the boy ... but at what cost? It would all come out—all the lies, his connection to the old man, and all the illegal contributions made to his campaign. The press would crucify him, and any hope he had of becoming a senator would be gone.

"Forget the boy. He's not your concern, and he's not why you're here. Look in the envelope."

Jeremy opened the envelope and emptied the contents onto the table.

"It's time to take things to the next level." The old man smiled. He knew he'd picked the right man for the job.

Jeremy flipped through the dossier from the envelope. He smiled as he realized what he was holding.

"Now that I have your undivided attention, can we get this meeting started? Take a seat Jeremy … or should I say, Senator Balile?"

Jeremy smiled as he reached for the chair.

Chapter One

Tiffany glanced out the window as she listened to the rain pounding against the glass. She wished she could have been home with her boys; in fact, she would rather have been anywhere else, but she knew that this was where she had to be in order to protect her son's interest.

She hated attending Triad meetings. They'd been great when she was young and rebellious; it had been something that she did with her then boyfriend, Alec, which set them apart from the other kids who attended their high school. The Triad was secretive and highly selective. The invitation to join had made her feel important at a time in her life when she had felt the most alienated.

Tiffany looked at her husband, Alec, sitting beside her. He was so engrossed in every word that was coming out of the director's mouth, it sickened her. She looked away. She had long suspected that the Triad was not the answer to the world's problems, as she had once believed. The more involved she got, the more she had become convinced that the leaders of the Triad had their own agenda, and that she and her family were no more than expendable pawns in their plans. They destroyed anyone and anything that stood in their way, and it frightened her. She could not understand why Alec couldn't see what had become so obvious to her, but she had given up trying to convince him. She would fight for their child's welfare alone, if necessary, no matter the personal cost, even if it was the last thing she did.

Tiffany felt everyone's eyes on her. Since she had rejected the Triad's selection of her son to become the "father of their future," they had all treated her like a traitor. Even Alec, who had supported her every decision since they were children, had sided with the Triad. He had considered the selection of their son an honor and could not understand her revulsion. Though disappointed by their reaction, she understood it. She, too, once had felt that the Triad could do no wrong. She had been all too happy to produce the child of prophesy, but now that she knew the truth, she could not close her eyes and pretend not to know.

The director ended all old business—that is, all old business except for the issue of her son. Tiffany sat straight up in her seat. This was why she had come.

"If there is nothing else, we'll open the floor for new business."

"What about my son? That issue hasn't been resolved. You tabled the matter last month and you promised—"

"The Triad has been informed about your concerns. Once a decision has been made, they will inform me, and I will inform you." The director was irritated by her interruptions. It had been a long day, and he was in no mood for Tiffany's ranting. He could not imagine why the Triad had not dealt with her before now, but he knew that it was not for him to question their infinite wisdom.

"That's not good enough." Tiffany heard her voice crack. "I'm only here as a courtesy to my husband, but my decision has been made. What we do with our son is not up to you, or them." She forced herself to swallow the lump in her throat. "He's our son. We'll decide."

"That is where you are mistaken. He does not belong to you. *You* don't even belong to you. We all belong to the master … or did you forget? Now sit down!"

Tiffany felt her knees buckle. She wanted to run, but her legs would not move. She forced herself to take several deep breaths to calm her nerves. She had to be strong for her son. She couldn't believe Alec had not defended her. Even worse, she could not believe that he was willing to consider allowing the destiny of their youngest son to be determined by the Triad.

Tiffany had made her own contingency plans in case the Triad refused to listen to reason. Her friend Sheila had introduced her to a Christian society known as the FLOCK (Followers of Christ's Kingdom), who had offered to help her escape with both of her sons, when and if she decided she was ready to make a complete break from the Triad. She knew that once made, there would be no going back. Every link to her previous life, including friends and loved ones, would be permanently severed. As difficult as living the rest of her life in exile would be, she knew that she had no other choice. She felt her window of opportunity closing, and she was not going to wait any longer. Tiffany had hoped that Alec would side with her and their family, but either way, she had made up her mind. Whatever Alec decided, she was not going to let them have her son.

"I don't want to be here," Tiffany whispered to Alec.

Alec continued to focus on what the director was saying and gave no indication that he had heard her.

"Did you hear me?" she hissed.

"This is not the place to discuss this." Alec looked around uncomfortably to see if anyone had noticed.

"Then tell me when, because you aren't hearing me," Tiffany retorted, her voice rising.

The Director stopped in midsentence. "Is everything okay?"

Tiffany gathered her things and walked toward the door. "I was just leaving."

"Wait," Alex called to her. Embarrassed, he rushed to join her. "I'm coming."

"With that, we are adjourned," the director said, dismissing the group. Then he called to Alec, who was trying to be as inconspicuous as possible. "Can I speak to you for a moment before you go?"

Alec froze in his tracks. Though he had never witnessed anything directly, he had heard of how the Triad handled those who fell out of favor with its elite, and he was frightened for his wife. He knew that she was worried about their son, Eric, spending so much time with the Triad and that she feared his being brainwashed, but he wished she wouldn't push so hard. He was just as worried as she was about Eric, but how could they deny their son the opportunity to become one of the Triad's elite? How could they deny him the benefits that such a position would afford him?

"Is she going to be okay?" The director patted Alec reassuringly on the shoulder.

"I'm working on it."

"Do you need help? I'd love the opportunity to speak to her, one on one. I can't imagine how difficult all this must be for her. In her eyes, he's her little boy, but to us, he's so much more."

"I'll talk to her. She just needs time." Alec tried to reassure the director.

"Unfortunately, that is a luxury we don't have."

"I'm sure she will listen to reason." Alec's pounding heart seemed as if it would burst out of his chest. He could feel the sweat dripping down his back.

"What about you?" asked the director.

"Me?"

"How are you handling all of this?" the director continued, his voice silken. "At best, this must feel a little strange."

"I'm … I'm doing just fine. I have faith."

"I hope you can pass a little of that faith on to your wife." The director knew that Tiffany was lost to them forever, even if Alec didn't.

"Yes. I do, too."

"Let me know if I can help," the director offered.

"I will. Thank you." Alec rushed to catch up with Tiffany.

The director watched as Alec and Tiffany left the parking lot before turning his attention to a young man waiting in the doorway. "Be careful." He instructed the young man. "Alec's a true believer, and I don't want him harmed. A boy needs his father."

"Yes, sir." The young man silently slipped out the door and jumped into a red SUV.

On the way home, Alec talked to Tiffany about the unyielding stance she'd taken.

"I've heard what they've had to say, and I don't believe it," Tiffany insisted. "If they want to worship our child, they'll have to do it from afar."

"How can you just discount everything you've heard? So far the prophesy has been accurate on every account. Eric is the One."

"No, he's our son, and I won't sacrifice him to this foolishness. I love you, but if you push me, I will leave you and take Eric and Neal with me." Tiffany hoped that her threats would force Alec to listen, but either way, she had made her decision. And if Alec refused to listen to reason, by that time the next day, his family would be gone.

"I will never allow anyone to take my children," Alec retorted, "not even you. I'd fight you tooth and nail for them."

"You'd lose," Tiffany said smugly. "All I would have to do is tell the court what you and those idiots have planned for my son." Her defiant tone took him off guard.

"You know as well as I do that the Triad's influence reaches far higher than our insignificant legal system. Besides, what makes you think they would even let this get to court?"

"If you know that they're dangerous, how can you entertain the thought of giving them control of our son?"

"They're not going to take him away. I don't understand the problem."

"The problem is that they want to control the destiny of our child, and I'm not okay with that."

"They would never harm Eric. He's too important to them."

"No. He's important to us. Their prophesy is important to them; following the wishes of the Triad is important to them. Eric is just a means to that end. If the Triad called for him to be sacrificed tomorrow, they would not hesitate. I would die before I let that happen." With Alec or without him, Tiffany promised herself, she and the boys were going. Her friend Sheila would be meeting her at the park the next morning, and she and her boys were going to escape the madness.

The Triad would try to find them—she knew that—but she had planned for every possible contingency. The FLOCK would hide them until new identities could be established. Maybe getting new identities was overkill, but if half of what she'd heard about Triad discipline was true, she feared it might not be enough.

"Did you hear me?" Alec's voice was harsh and irritated. He hated when she made unilateral decisions concerning the boys.

Tiffany shook her head. "I'm sorry; I'm just tired. What did you say?"

"You don't get to make all of the decisions. Don't forget he's my son, too. Don't you think I want what's best for him? Don't you think I love him just as much as you do?"

"I think you've been blinded by your adoration of the Triad. You've allowed yourself to be manipulated. They're dangerous. Tell me you don't see that."

"They're believers," Alec insisted.

"No, they're fanatics, and I'm going to protect our son from them, even if you—"

Their brakes screeched suddenly as Alec swerved to miss an oncoming car. He clutched the wheel tightly; trying to regain control of the vehicle, but the car was rammed by the red SUV and slammed into the ditch.

Alec touched his chest and winced. The seatbelt's tight grip and the blow from the airbag likely had bruised him. As his thoughts cleared, he checked on Tiffany. She was no longer sitting beside him—her seatbelt had not held. Alec crawled out of the car. His chest hurt, but the greater pain was the sinking feeling in the pit of his stomach that warned him not to look in the ditch.

Neal was asleep at home when he received the call informing him of his parents' accident. He dressed and woke his little brother. As they drove to the hospital, Neal reassured Eric that their parents would be okay, but in reality, he was worried. The caller had been unable to give him much information, other than that an ambulance had been called, and there had been at least one major injury.

When the boys arrived at the hospital, they found their father in the waiting room, talking to a police officer. Alec motioned for them to join him. Neal was relieved that his father seemed okay, but he worried that he did not see his mother. Eric ran to embrace his father.

"Based on the witness accounts at the scene, you have nothing to worry about. I will inform you once my investigation is complete." The officer handed Alec his card. "If you have any questions, or if you remember anything, please don't hesitate to call me."

"Thank you."

The officer smiled at Eric who was tightly holding his father's leg. "Are these your boys?"

"They are." Alec ruffled Eric's hair.

"Take it easy." The officer handed Alec a copy of the accident report.

"Thanks again. I'll call you if I remember anything else." Alec watched the officer leave before turning his attention to his sons.

"The person who called us said that there was a major injury," Neal reported.

His father nodded. "The driver of the car that hit us was killed."

"Where's Mom?" Eric asked. He loved his father, but he adored his mother.

"They want to keep her for observation, but I just spoke to her, and she seemed fine to me. We'll come back tomorrow to see her."

"I want to see her now!" Eric demanded.

"The doctors gave her something to help her sleep. They said we can see her tomorrow."

Alec took his sons home.

****

As Tiffany lay in the bed, trying not to imagine the worst, she contemplated her options. She had to get out of the hospital and get back to her boys. She was their best chance for survival, and nothing was going to stop her from protecting them.

"Tiffany," Sheila whispered. "Are you awake?"

Tiffany turned to see her friend Shelia peeking around her room door. "Yes. I'm so glad you came." She smiled.

"I came as soon as I got your message. We were worried when you didn't show up at the park yesterday." Shelia hugged Tiffany. She was so happy to find her friend alive and safe. She had waited for Tiffany for hours, and had feared the worse when she did not arrive at the designated time.

"I would have called you sooner, but Alec has been here most of the day. He's so worried about me."

"Do you feel your son will be safe until you get home? Do you trust Alec?"

"I really do. Alec has been great. He has promised not to allow anything to happen concerning Eric unless we both agree."

"How about you? Do you feel safe here?" Sheila asked.

"What's that suppose to mean? Do you think that I'm in danger? Do you think that they set us up?"

"Don't you? Look at the facts. You confront them, and then you're in a horrific accident. You car was brand new, and what? *Your* seatbelt was the one that malfunctioned? Your husband walks away with barely a scratch, and you wind up on your back in the hospital. You tell me. Do you feel safe?"

"I hadn't thought about it."

"You have to be careful. They're playing for keeps, and you have far too much at stake."

"I know that you're right." Tiffany agreed. She reached into her side table and grabbed a pen and paper. She wrote Alec a letter, telling him that if anything happened to her, she needed to know that he would see the Triad for what it was; she needed to know that he would protect their son.

"If anything happens to me," Tiffany said to Sheila, "I want you to give this to my husband, and then I want you to save my boys."

****

"How is she?" the director asked his assistant about Tiffany's health.

"Dr. Phillips says she's getting stronger every day. He's running out of excuses for keeping her in the hospital," the assistant explained.

"That's too bad. I had hoped not to have to involve him further. He spooks easily, and this requires finesse."

"He understands what must be done."

"Yes, but send someone else. Tiffany and Tory are pretty close, and since Tory's a nurse at Mercy Hospital, she should be able to get close enough to take care of matters without raising suspicions."

"Tory doesn't work on Tiffany's floor anymore, but Phillips can personally request that she be assigned to Tiffany. It makes sense. Like you said, they are so close," the assistant agreed. "It's perfect."

"Make it happen," the director ordered.

****

"You have to get me out of here," Tiffany whispered so that Neal and Eric would not hear them.

"Dr. Phillips says that you can come home in a couple of days," Alec reassured her.

"I'm fine. I've already been here for five days. They've run enough tests. I need to get home to my boys."

"I promised I wouldn't entertain anything concerning Eric until you were up on your feet," he whispered. "Neal, will you take your brother to get a soda?"

Tiffany looked into Alec's eyes. She wanted to believe him; she *did* believe him. It was the rest of them that she didn't trust. "I need to go home. I don't feel safe here."

"Now you're just being paranoid."

"Did you know that they increased my meds?"

"Why?"

"Exactly!"

"No, I mean, why is that suspicious to you?"

"If I'm getting better, shouldn't they be decreasing my meds?"

"I'm sure that they know what they are doing. If Dr. Phillips increased your medication, it has to have been for a good reason."

"Maybe I wouldn't be so paranoid if people weren't acting so suspicious. I woke up around midnight, and I found Tory standing over my IV."

"Maybe, she was here because she is your new nurse. Dr. Phillips thought you'd enjoy the company of someone you know."

"I don't trust her."

"You're friends."

"She's one of them."

"You use to be one of them as well. Does that make you dangerous?" Alec felt that she was worrying unnecessarily, but he wanted her to be happy. "I'll ask Dr. Phillips to assign you a new nurse."

"Thank you."

"Hi Alec."

Alec and Tiffany turned to see Tory standing in the doorway. They worried that she might have overheard them; however, she gave no indication that she had heard their conversation.

The boys returned, carrying their sodas. Eric hopped onto the bed. Tiffany kissed his forehead. She was prepared to take on the entire world to save him, if necessary.

"Okay, boys, it's time to give Mom some rest," Tory said, interrupting their family moment. She ruffled Eric's hair. "Don't worry. I'll take excellent care of your mommy."

"When are you coming home, Mommy?"

"Dr. Phillips says I can go home in two days."

"I'll check on what we discussed." Alec promised.

Neal hugged her. "Bye mom."

"I miss you." Eric waved.

"I miss you more." Tiffany blew her son a kiss as she watched her family leave.

"This will help you sleep," Tory explained as she injected the contents of a vial she was carrying in her pocket.

"I really don't need any help in that regard. All I seem to do …" Tiffany's voice trailed off as the drugs reached her system.

"How long will it take?" a voice from the doorway asked.

What was that? Tiffany thought. The voice sounded eerily familiar, but she could not quite make it out. She struggled to open her eyes.

"This should only take a few minutes," Tory reassured the man, who had quietly slipped into the room. He had been careful not to be seen by Tiffany's family as they left her room.

A few minutes to do what? Tiffany wondered. Suddenly, she felt tightness in her chest that made it difficult for her to breath. She tried to get Tory's attention. She opened her mouth, but no sound would escape.

"Are you sure this drug will be untraceable? What if there is an autopsy?"

"Some of the test results will reveal unusually high levels of certain hormones, but the only way to detect this drug is to test for it specifically, and why would they do that? There probably won't even be an autopsy. She simply relapsed in the middle of the night and succumbed to her injuries. It happens all the time."

Tiffany finally recognized the voice. *Why is the director checking on me?* she wondered as she drew her final breath.

****

"I'm sorry, Alec. There was nothing more we could do." Dr. Phillips tried to explain Tiffany's death.

Alec collapsed into his seat. "I don't believe you. She was getting better. I know she was."

"She was, but apparently the damage done to her internal system was just too extensive."

"I want an autopsy."

"That's your right, but I feel you'll just be putting yourself and your family though additional stress and pain for no reason. I just don't know what an autopsy can possibly tell us that we don't already know."

"It can prove that she was poisoned."

"I see. Did something happen that would make you believe that there may have been foul play?" Phillips pressed.

"I cannot go into matters right now. I just want the truth."

"I understand. Let me make the arrangements."

****

Sheila reached into her pocket and removed the envelope. She had read the letter several times since Tiffany's death and had pondered what she should do with it. She had made a vow to Tiffany to give her husband the letter and to save her friend's child from the Triad. Helping Tiffany escape with the children was one thing; taking Eric herself was kidnapping. Sheila felt both conflicted and inadequate for the task, so she prayed for guidance.

She remembered the day she had first met Tiffany. They both had shown up early for their boys' baseball tryouts and had struck up a conversation to help pass the time. They had been thrilled when both their boys were placed on the same team. They spent the entire season talking about everything from raising children to which drugstore filled prescriptions the fastest.

Even though Tiffany enjoyed the opportunity to talk to someone who saw her son as just a normal child, it had taken almost the entire season before she had found the courage to share her real concerns about Eric with Sheila. She had sat idly by as her son Neal was indoctrinated into the society. She'd been so young when he was born, and she, like so many others, labored under the illusion that the Triad could do no wrong. She'd pretended not to notice the disturbing changes in Neal's personality. She couldn't bear watching the same thing happen to Eric.

To Tiffany's surprise, Sheila knew all about the Triad. She warned Tiffany that her concerns were valid and that she had to do something soon if she wanted to protect her son. Sheila had shared about her family's own experiences with the Triad and their narrow escape one cold winter night. She told Tiffany about how her parents had been recruited in college and about how they had been raised under the Triad's iron fist. Her parents had both been devout members until she had been selected to be sacrificed. Tiffany had asked what gave her parents the courage to run. That was the first time Sheila felt led to tell her friend about her faith in Jesus, and about the organization that had saved her life, the FLOCK.

Sheila was confident that she would see her good friend again in heaven, but now she had to focus on Eric and Neal. Their souls had been very precious to their mother and even more so to God. She couldn't fail them. She placed the letter in Alec's mailbox and returned home to wait for his call.

****

Dr. Phillips handed the autopsy report to the young director's assistant.

"The Triad appreciates all that you have done. If this information had fallen into the wrong hands, it could have posed a good deal of problems for the Triad. There would have been an investigation, at the very least, and it is important that we do not lose the support of the father. The son is still too young and will need a strong male role model."

"What about the brother? How old is he now?" Phillips asked.

"Neal will be eighteen in a few weeks. He is still an option, but we would rather regain the father's support. Eric has just lost his mother, and the Triad fears the lost of his father so soon could cost us the trust of the child. We don't know what suspicions the father may have shared with Eric, and it's a risk we would rather not take unless there is no other choice."

"What if the damage can't be repaired? Why does it have to be this family, this boy? It just seems like they are more trouble than they're worth. Anyone else would have been honored. Why not just select a more worthy, cooperative family? There are over twenty others to choose from."

"It is not for us to question the master's will."

"That was not my intention." Phillips shuffled uncomfortably. "I would never—"

"Don't worry. I didn't think you would."

"The new autopsy report should support my original findings that death was the result of complications arising from injuries sustained in the accident."

"Should? That's not good enough."

"I'm sure it will hold up to the strictest scrutiny."

"What about the nurse who saw the original report?" the man asked.

"I know this girl. She's fine. I can get her to back off. She thinks that I walk on water." Phillips laughed uncomfortably. He fully appreciated the precarious position that he found himself. His assistant, Karen, should never have had the opportunity to see the original report. He'd been careless, and the Triad had very little patience for incompetence. He knew that if the Triad decided he was too unreliable, he might find himself on the other side of an autopsy.

"That may be, but the Triad is not willing to take that chance."

"What do they want me to do about it?"

"Don't worry. They will handle everything." After he left Phillips' office, the young assistant placed a call to the director.

"Are you sure Karen hasn't told anyone?" The director asked.

"No, I'm not."

"I want her questioned beforehand."

"I'll make the arrangements."

"No, I want you to handle this personally."

"What about Dr. Phillips?" the man asked. "This mistake rests fully on his shoulders."

The Director tapped his fingers on the arm of his chair as he contemplated his options. "Let him go. He has not worn out his usefulness."

****

Once again, Alec sat in Dr. Phillips' office to discuss his wife's unexpected death. Dr. Phillips removed the autopsy report from his desk. Alec listened as the doctor first explained the complications that had resulted in Tiffany's untimely death, and then as he explained the mix-up that led to her unfortunate cremation. Phillips' explanation seemed plausible, but it still felt wrong. Though there was nothing tangible to suggest foul play; it was all just a little too convenient for Alec's comfort. Alec felt as if his world had ended. He tried to hand the report back to Dr. Phillips.

"That's your copy."

Alec held the report against his chest as if it contained his wife's final essence. He could not believe that he would never see her again.

"I'm sorry about the mix-up."

"I still don't understand how this could have happened."

"When you signed for the autopsy to be performed, in your understandably distressed state, you must have inadvertently marked the box to have the remains cremated afterwards." He handed Alec a copy of the authorization form he had signed.

Alec fought back the tears. Tiffany had been his world, and he had failed her miserably. Maybe Dr. Phillips was right. Maybe he was seeing conspiracies everywhere because it was what he needed to see. If Tiffany had been murdered, then it wasn't his incompetence that had cost him the only woman he had ever loved. But that wasn't the case. It had been raining all day, and he should have driven more carefully; he should have slowed down. Maybe he secretly hoped that she had been murdered, because the alternative—that it was his fault she was dead—was just too unbearable.

"She wanted to be buried next to her parents."

"She still can. I'll arrange for her ashes to be returned to you before you leave. Nurse Agnes will take you to sign the release papers."

"Thank you." Alec shook the doctor's hand and followed the nurse into the hall.

After Alec singed the papers, Agnes left him to retrieve his wife's remains.

"Excuse me, sir," a young nurse whispered as Agnes walked out of sight. "My name is Karen, and I worked with Dr. Phillips on your wife's case."

"Yes, I remember you."

"I think you should have this." She handed him a folder. "Dr. Phillips removed these results from your wife's final autopsy report. He doesn't know that I kept them. He thinks that they have been destroyed, but I felt you should have them. Some of your wife's levels were higher than you would usually find in a woman in her condition. Taken alone, it doesn't prove anything, but taking your concerns into account, they can be seen as somewhat suspicious. I understand why, with all the problems surrounding your wife's case, Dr. Phillips would have wanted to protect your family from any further pain, but I'm not comfortable with altering records. I just ask that you try to keep my name out of things if this goes any further."

"I'll do my best, but I know that my wife didn't just die, and I don't plan to let her death go uninvestigated. I may have failed to protect her in life, but I won't fail her again." He took the folder from the young nurse and waited for Agnes to return with his wife's remains.

As Alec returned home, he could not stop thinking about all the times Tiffany had asked him for his support. Their final conversation replayed over and over again in his head. There were so many things he could have, should have done differently. He wrestled with what he should do. He still had the boys' well-being to consider. He wanted to contact the police, but he knew that the Triad had members on the force, and if the Triad had killed his wife, there was no telling what they would do to him—and then his boys would be left alone and unprotected.

As Alec pulled into the driveway, he grabbed his mail before heading into the house. He found the letter from Tiffany and the note from Sheila with her phone number. After reading Tiffany's letter, he put it into his pocket next to his heart and picked up the phone to call Sheila.

"Hello, Sheila speaking," the woman answered.

"This is Alec. We need to meet."

****

"How is your father handling things at home?" The director asked.

"Not well. He blames himself for my mother's death." Neal explained.

"You were wise to come to see me." The director motioned for Neal to sit across from him.

"You said that I should keep my eyes open for anything suspicious." Neal sat in the chair. It was uncomfortably firm, but he pretended not to notice. He glanced around the office at all the civic awards the director had accumulated.

The director smiled. "Quite impressive, huh?"

"Yes, sir."

"You see that one?" The director pointed to a small medal encased in glass.

"Yes, sir." Neal read the inscription. "For Bravery Above And Beyond the Call Of Duty."

"It was given to me by the president himself." He took the medal from its case and handed it to Neal. "It's my favorite. Do you know why?"

"Is it because the president presented it to you?"

"No. It's because of what it cost me personally."

"I don t understand."

"Sometimes we are called upon to make difficult choices. Sometimes duty requires us to make sacrifices. Do you understand?"

"Yes, sir." Neal lowered his head. His shoulders slumped from the weight of the burden that rested upon them.

"Do you know what your duty is?"

"Yes, sir." Neal lifted his head. "My duty is to protect the chosen one."

****

"What do you know about the history of the Triad?" Sheila asked.

"I know that there were three original Triad members, and that they were selected to be the keepers of the prophesy." Alec's patience was already wearing thin. He wanted to know what any of this had to do with his wife's death.

"I would like to tell you a story."

"What does this have to do with—"

"If you would humor me for a brief moment, I think you'll understand," Shelia begged. When Alec agreed, Sheila continued. "Thousands of years ago, the three daughters of a merchant were approached by a traveler. He promised them power beyond anything they could imagine, if they would serve him. As proof of their loyalty, after one year, each would be required to present him with a token of their complete dedication. Each agreed, and for one year, each sister prospered beyond her imagination.

"After one year, the sisters prepared for the return of the traveler. The first sister had married a farmer, and their crops and livestock outnumbered all of their neighbors. To honor the traveler, she presented him with one-third of all that they had. The traveler was impressed, and he promised that her family would continue to prosper. The second sister had married a merchant of the finest linen in all the land. To show her loyalty, she presented him with the finest of all her husband's linen and half of their servants. The traveler promised that she, too, would continue to be rewarded.

The third sister had married a man of great power, and he ruled over many. They had much land and even more servants than both of her sisters. She, however, did not present the traveler with land or money. She did not offer him male servants or female servants. To prove her complete devotion, she offered their best. She presented him with their firstborn son, her husband's only heir, as a sacrifice. It is said that the traveler was so impressed by her that he promised her that from her lineage, a god would be born, and that the descendants of her sisters would kneel before him. The child would have such unimaginable power that he could wage war with God himself. It was said that this child would be born to rule over the entire world and that his followers would rule with him."

"You think they believe that Eric is this child?" Alec asked.

"No. They believe he will be his father."

Alec had listened with a healthy sense of skepticism. "It sounds like you know a lot about the Triad."

"More than I would like." Shelia was uncomfortable about revealing too much about her history to someone she barely knew. She would rather have waited until they had time to learn to trust each other, but time was not a luxury they could afford. "The direct descendants of those three sisters form the three houses of the Triad elite. To honor the third sister's act of sacrifice, every twenty years one of the houses is chosen; and from that house, a family is chosen; and from that family, a child is selected to be sacrificed."

"How do you know so much? Were you a member?"

"About twenty-six years ago, I was the child selected to be sacrificed."

****

"We need to do something before things get out of control." Having learned of Karen's betrayal, Dr. Phillips was terrified.

"I'm afraid things have already gone too far. I had hoped that this matter could be resolved without any further tragedy, but Alec's become a real problem," the director explained. "The Triad is aware of everything and has made its decision. The matter is being handled as we speak."

"What about the nurse?"

"She is no longer your concern."

****

Alec could not stop thinking about his meeting with Shelia. He replayed it over and over until he felt his head would burst. The more he thought about things, the more he began to understand Tiffany's panic. If they would sacrifice their own children, what chance did Eric have? Tiffany had been right all along. There was no way he could entrust their son's well-being to the Triad.

Paranoia began to take hold as Alec drove home after speaking with Sheila. He checked his rearview mirror for the hundredth time. He and Shelia had made arrangements to sneak Eric out of the state, and he wouldn't relax until Eric was safely in the hands of the FLOCK

They feared Neal might have already been seduced by the Triad; so they decided to keep their plans from the teen until after Eric was safe. He and Neal could join Eric after they were sure where Neal's loyalties rested. He also planned to warn Karen that she might also be in danger. She'd gone out on a limb to confide in him, and he felt it was the least he owed her.

****

When Neal arrived home, the phone was ringing. The caller ID listed the call as coming from his father's cell phone. He rushed to grab it before the answering machine picked up.

"Hello. This is Officer McKinney."

"This is Neal. You are calling from my father's cell phone."

"Is your mother available?"

"My mother died. It's just my father, my brother, and I. Is there a problem?"

"I am here at the Jericho Inn on the corner of First Street and Echo Drive. There has been an incident. We have your little brother, and we need someone to come to retrieve him."

"Where is my father?"

Officer McKinney paused and took a deep breath. There was no easy way to tell someone that a family member was dead. He would have much rather to have spoken to Neal in person. "I'm sorry to inform you that he's deceased."

"Is my brother okay?"

"He's a little confused about why we're here and where his father is. He was asleep in the room next to where we found the body, and he still doesn't know about the incident."

"Please don't tell him anything. I'll be right there."

Neal hung up the phone and pulled on his jacket. He steadied his nerves for what he knew was going to be one of the most difficult things he had ever had to do in his life, telling his brother about the death of their father.

Officer McKinney was surprised that Neal had not asked more questions. It was his experience that most people could not stop asking questions upon hearing that a family member has died unexpectedly. Neal hadn't seemed at all surprised by the news. He hadn't even asked how his father had died.

He'd only seemed concerned about the little boy. McKinney made a mental note of his suspicions.

"Officer McKinney." A young officer interrupted his train of thought.

"Yes. What is it?"

"There is another body."

"Here?"

"No, sir, across town. She's been identified as a young nurse named Karen Archer."

"What does she have to do with my case?"

"I checked our victim's cell phone history and her number was the last call he made. I called the number and an officer from downtown answered. He said their victim has been dead for less than two hours."

Officer McKinney glanced around the room. All the evidence suggested that Alec had committed suicide. "Is there any chance that she committed suicide?"

"Not unless she tortured herself first."

McKinney didn't know what to make of things. The medical examiners had put both Karen's and Alec's times of death at roughly the same time, and since Karen's body had been found at least an hour away, there was no way their victim could have caused her death.

"I guess there is no chance that this is a coincidence." McKinney commented.

"I wouldn't count on it."

No, that would have been too easy. There was definitely more to this case than first met the eye. "Be careful." He warned another officer. "We can't afford to miss anything. Something tells me that this case is going to cost us many sleepless nights."

Chapter Two

Eric was excited when he opened his college acceptance letter. He shared the letter with Sarah. She was an old friend of his mother's who had taken him and his brother, Neal, into her home after their parents died. Both he and Neal felt extremely close to her. She had been their champion since their parents' death and was all the family they had. Neither Eric nor Neal had ever met their parents' families. Their mother was an only child, and both of her parents were dead; their father had been estranged from his parents since leaving home at age sixteen to be with their mother. When their grandparents had sought to send Eric away to a private school after the tragic death of their father, Sarah had fought hard to win custody to keep the boys together. It had been Sarah who introduced him to the Triad shortly after the death of their parents and who later encouraged Eric to apply to the Triad for a full scholarship, which made it possible for him to even consider attending college full time. Next to each other, Sarah was the most important person in Neal and Eric's life.

Sarah was thrilled that Eric would be attending college nearby. She had never felt the closeness she shared with Eric with her own children. She considered being entrusted with the future of the Triad a real honor. She knew that the Triad would be pleased.

Eric couldn't wait to share the news with his brother, but he knew that he would have to wait until Neal called that weekend, as Neal was on deployment. He understood Neal's decision to join the military to help support them, but he didn't have to like it.

The doorbell rang, and Eric rushed to answer it. It was his best friends Aaron and Christopher. They were both holding their own acceptance letters. The only thing better than being accepted to NYU was being accepted to NYU with both his best friends. The boys decided to go out to celebrate.

"Let me grab my coat from upstairs." Aaron and Christopher followed Eric to his bedroom to grab a jacket.

"So what are you doing Sunday?" Aaron asked matter-of-factly.

"Nothing important."

"Now you are."

"Let me guess, you guys want me to go with you to church again."

"Don't pretend that you didn't have a great time last Sunday," Christopher teased.

"Yeah, but—"

"But nothing. Did you have a good time or not?" Aaron demanded. He couldn't understand why Sarah and Neal had such a problem with Eric's exploring Christianity, but he wasn't going to let that stop him from sharing his faith with his good friend.

"Yes. I was surprised. It was nothing like Sarah and Neal said it would be."

"So does that mean you're coming?"

"I'm there."

Eric heard the door downstairs open. Sarah called to him from the bottom of the stairs. He could tell by her voice that something was horribly wrong. He rushed downstairs.

"Eric, I'm so sorry. It's your brother." Sarah took his hand in hers and led him into the living room, where there were two naval officials waiting.

"It is my duty to inform you that your brother was killed at 0900 hours. That would be 9:00 AM civilian time," the naval officer explained.

"Can you tell me how this happened? He wasn't even supposed to be in harm's way." Eric felt as if all the air had been sucked from the room.

"It was a training accident," the naval officer explained.

"I want to see him."

"That would not be advisable. You see, there was a fire." Sarah explained. Her words were barely above a whisper, but to Eric they were deafening. He didn't feel his legs as they buckled from beneath him. The officer and Sarah helped him to the sofa. Sarah rushed to get a damp cloth from the bathroom.

"It's going to be okay," she promised.

Eric blinked his eyes. He could see her lips moving, but he couldn't hear the words.

"Is there something we can do?" Aaron asked from the hall.

"No. He'll be fine. It's just going to take some time. We'll take care of him. You should go home. I'll have him to call you when he's feeling better."

As Aaron and Christopher reluctantly turned to leave, Christopher glanced back at their friend. He wished he knew what to say. He couldn't imagine losing a close family member, yet Eric had lost three.

****

Aaron's father's heart broke for his son's friend. He'd only met Eric a few times, but he knew that Eric had been orphaned at a young age. He couldn't imagine how the death of his brother was going to affect him, but he knew that Neal had been all that Eric had left. At Aaron's request, his father reached out to their church for assistance. Pastor Campbell was happy to help and offered the church's cemetery as a final resting place.

At first, Sarah had rejected the offer, but the director thought it might be a good idea. He felt it might play right into their plans, as Eric would be forced to deal with the contradictions between a loving God and unimaginable loss.

Eric stood motionless as he watched Neal's casket being lowered into the ground. Thoughts of his father's funeral flooded his mind. He remembered how frightened and alone he had felt, but Neal had helped him through each agonizing moment. He remembered feeling Neal squeeze his hand comfortingly as they turned to leave.

Eric listened as Pastor Campbell read scriptures. He wished he could find comfort in the words, but in truth, all he felt was anger. He felt anger for the loss of his family and anger for being left alone, but most of all, he felt anger because he had wanted so much to believe in a divine order and a benevolent God. He promised that day at his brother's graveside that he would do better, go farther, and accomplish more, because all his accomplishments would have to be for both himself and his brother.

Neal watched his funeral from a building across the street. Even from this distance, he could see the pain in Eric's eyes, and for the first time he questioned the wisdom of the Triad.

"I did this to him." Neal blinked away a tear.

"You did this *for* him." Balile insisted.

"I still don't understand why this is necessary. It seems so cruel, and it could backfire. He might never forgive us—or worse, we could drive him right into the arms of those fanatics."

"When the time is right, we will explain everything to him, and he will understand that there was no other way. Would you rather let them brainwash your brother, just like they did your mother? Believing you're dead may hurt him now, but if they get their hands on him, they'll destroy him." Balile patted Neal reassuringly on the shoulder. He understood how difficult this was going to be for his young protégé, but they were all subject to the will of the Triad, and if the Triad felt this was the answer, who were they to question?

"Eric's not a child anymore. If we just explained to him how dangerous his newfound friendship with this pastor is and how Christianity is an affront to everything we believe, he'll understand. He'd never fall for their deception. He's too smart for that." Neal pleaded his and Eric's case. He couldn't believe there was no other way.

"Your mother was one of the smartest women I'd ever met, but even she was susceptible. Pastor Campbell is a very charismatic leader. How long do you think it would take for him to brainwash your brother? This is the only way to put a permanent end to this God business. The Triad believes that your death will lead your brother to not only reject Christianity but even the possibility of the existence of a just and benevolent God. It will help him to choose a more enlightened path."

"What happens when he discovers our deception? Won't he reject us as well?"

"We hope that he will be old enough to make a more rational decision. Right now, the influence this pastor exerts over your brother is unnatural. Eric is looking for a father figure, and the pastor is using that to lead Eric astray."

"If this preacher is the problem, why not just get rid of him?" Neal asked. It seemed so simple to him.

"As long as Eric is seeking, there will always be another Pastor Campbell to help him find his way."

"I still can't believe there was no other way."

"Faith and obedience for now, and understanding will come later," Balile promised. "We should go. Our plane leaves in two hours."

Neal couldn't take his eyes off of his brother. He watched as Sarah and Eric's car drove out of sight.

"It's not forever, right?"

"Nothing is forever," Balile promised.

****

"I just wanted to stop by to say thank you for attending my brother's funeral. It was kind of you and your congregation to be so supportive," Eric told Pastor Campbell. He wasn't a member of their church, and they'd had no obligation to attend. Their support had meant a lot to him.

"If there is anything we can do, please, please let us know," Pastor Campbell offered. Though Eric had only recently started visiting Pastor

Campbell's church, the pastor recognized that this was a critical moment for the young man.

"I'll be fine."

"I know you will, but still, if you need anything ...."

"Thank you for the offer, but I've got everything under control. I've got a full scholarship for college, my parents left my brother and me the house, and I'll get a check from the military for my brother. Money is not going to be a problem. It looks like I have everything covered."

"That's good to hear, but I also meant if you needed to talk. There are those who say that I'm a really good listener."

Eric appreciated the sentiment, but he was in no mood to talk to anyone, least of all about faith. Faith had never served him or his family. Losing his only brother had left him numb. He and Neal had been very close.

"I want you to know that we're all praying for you, and we can't wait to see you back at church."

"Thanks, anyway. I know you mean well, but I don't think I'm going to be coming back to church. I start school in the fall, and I plan to be too busy, so don't waste your prayers on me. I won't need them."

"Don't make such an important decision out of anger. You're relationship with God is the most important decision you will ever have to make. I understand you need time to heal, but God can—"

"God? I'm sorry, but you're preaching to the wrong person. It was wonderful imagining that there was an omniscient being out there watching out for me, but I don't have time for such trivial imaginations anymore. How did you put it? 'When I was a child, I acted like a child, but when I became grown, I put away my childish ways.' My brother would say that it was high time that I grew up, wouldn't you?"

"I know that you're angry and confused right now."

"I'm not angry or confused. Crap happens; what are you going to do about it? It's no one's fault. I don't blame God, because I don't believe in your God. I tried to give your religion a try, and it just didn't work for me, but don't feel bad. It's not you. Religion is not for everyone."

"Yes, you're right. Religion is not for everyone, but God is."

"If I believed in your God, I'd have to wonder why he cares so much about sparrows and so little about the rest of us. Maybe I'd ask him why he has it in for me and mine. I'd love to know where he was when my mom died from an accident that he could have stopped, or when my dad killed himself because he couldn't forgive himself for killing the only woman he ever loved? I would settle for just knowing where he was when my brother died too young, just because he devoted his life to doing the right thing."

Pastor Campbell knew that there was nothing he could say at that moment to make things better or to relieve Eric's pain. Eric was so blinded by his anger that he was in no mood to hear anything, so Pastor Campbell just listened to him and prayed that Eric would one day find his way back to the God who loved him and who was the only one who could give Eric the peace he so desperately needed. "I know that you've had a rough time of it, and the tendency might be to want to blame someone."

"Losing both my parents before puberty definitely altered my perspective on things, but you're wrong. I don't blame anyone, and I certainly can't blame a God in whom I don't believe, and believe me, that's a good thing. If there were a God, he'd sure as heck have a lot of explaining to do."

Pastor Campbell watched as Eric left the church for what he feared was the last time.

Chapter Three

Holidays, birthdays—now add graduations to the list of days that Eric hated. He knew all the "psycho mumbo-jumbo" about why special occasions were so difficult for him, but that did not make the days go by any easier. He was a man now, and he felt that it was long past time that he put his past behind him, but there he was again, brooding over what he'd lost.

Eric glanced at the clock above the bar. He swirled the lone remaining bits of ice in his drink before downing the last few drops; then he glanced at the clock again.

"Can I get you another drink while you wait for your friends?"

"Yeah, that'll be good. It's getting crowded, so I'm going to grab a table. Can you make it a double this time and send it to my table?"

The bartender nodded.

Eric felt a hand on his shoulder. "Sorry we're late," Christopher apologized as he plopped down on one of the seats. "We were heading out the door when Mitch called. He and Laura won't be here until just in time for graduation. Do you know what that means?"

"You can get smashed and still have half the day tomorrow to sober up before your folks get here?" Eric shook his head in mock disgust. "Do you condone this behavior, or should I say, misbehavior?"

"Not at all," joked Aaron as he grabbed the last seat.

"Can I get you boys anything?" their waitress, Jennifer, asked placing the double vodka in front of Eric.

"Thanks." Eric smiled at her.

"I see you started without us," Christopher protested, eyeing the drink.

"I guess you have some catching up to do."

"Then I better get started." Christopher turned to Jennifer. "I'll have what he's having."

"And what can I get you?" Jennifer focused her attention on Aaron. "No, let me guess. You'd like a club soda."

"Thanks. Oh, and—"

"Lemon, no lime, right?" She winked and went to place the orders.

"Am I that predictable?" Aaron blushed. He tried to hide his feelings, but he was sure that his friends suspected that he and Jennifer were dating. He and his friends loved to hang out and rate their dates, but Jennifer was special, and he wasn't ready for their scrutiny.

"I order the same thing each week, too. She didn't remember my drink," Christopher protested.

Aaron noticed the message light flashing on his cell phone.

"Is anything wrong?" Christopher asked.

"Be right back. I need to return a call." Aaron excused himself.

"Whatever, dude." Eric shook his head. He knew the call was from Aaron's parents. He turned his attention to Christopher's parents. "So, are you picking up Mitch and Laura?"

"No. I told them that I had some last-minute details to take care of before graduation, so my dad's renting a car."

"What last minute details?" Eric looked bewildered.

"Ironing my tie." Christopher laughed.

"You didn't tell him that did you?"

"I'm irreverent, not stupid. I know who pays the bills."

"Yeah, and you better not forget it."

"Don't worry; there's no way Mitch would ever let me do that."

"They mean well."

"No, they don't."

"I know." Eric laughed. "Your dad reminds me why I'm glad I don't have one."

"Thanks a lot, dude."

"Any time."

Aaron returned.

"Back so soon?" Eric's tone dripped with sarcasm, but Aaron pretended not to notice.

"My parents weren't there." Aaron explained. "I left a message."

"So when are the 'Cleavers' getting into town?"

Eric was never subtle in his ridicule of Aaron and the closeness he and his family shared. Aaron usually just tried to ignore it, but sometimes it did get under his skin.

"My parents should be here in another eight hours, thirty minutes, and …" Aaron made an exaggerated display of pretending to examine an invisible watch. "…eighteen seconds."

"Think you can be more specific?" Christopher laughed, trying to ease the mounting tension between the two friends.

Eric motioned for Jennifer, and he and Christopher ordered another drink.

"Can I get you something else to drink to help get you through the night with these two?" she teased Aaron.

"Of course not," Eric answered for him. "His mommy and daddy are coming to town, and Saint Aaron wouldn't dare disappoint them."

"I'm good. Someone has to make sure these guys make it home okay."

"You just always have to be the responsible one," Eric mumbled, but again, Aaron pretended not to notice.

Aaron tried to be empathetic. He knew how hard things had been for Eric when he was growing up. Sarcasm had become almost an involuntary defense mechanism to help him cope with a tragic life. He had so much to overcome, first with the death of his parents and then the tragic loss of his brother. No one could blame Eric for being a little bitter. Sometimes life could seem so unfair, so random, but Aaron imagined that to Eric, life must have seemed to have it in for him personally.

Aaron's cell phone rang. It was his parents, returning his call.

"Hello!" Aaron yelled into the phone. "I can't hear you over the music. Let me call you right back!" Aaron headed toward the door.

"Why do you have to be such a jerk to him?" Christopher confronted Eric once Aaron had gone.

"What are you talking about? You're just drunk."

"Yes. I may be drunk, but I'm not deaf or blind."

"What's that suppose to mean?" Eric asked. He could not believe Christopher was siding with Aaron.

"I know vodka ain't the only thing that is making you green tonight."

"Aaron knows how I get. He knows that I was only joking. He doesn't take me seriously, and neither do you, usually," Eric said, dismissing Christopher's accusation.

"No, you weren't just joking. That may float with someone who doesn't know you so well, but don't hand me that crap."

"I didn't mean anything by it. I just get a little carried away when I've had a few."

"Oh, please. You're not that drunk yet. Lying to me is stupid, but lying to yourself is pathetic."

Eric was a master at hiding his emotions. He just wrapped them in so many layers of sarcasm that even he couldn't recognize them. He pretended to be unaffected by his friend's reproach, but Christopher knew that he'd hit a nerve.

"Aaron's childhood may have been sickeningly sweet compared to ours, and yes, he can really be annoyingly perfect, but he's a good guy and a better friend than either of us deserve. I seem to remember his saving your sorry tail more than a few times." Christopher rested his head on his arm.

Aaron returned to the table to find both Christopher and Eric significantly more intoxicated than before he left.

"Hey, dude. What took you so long?" Christopher slurred, and plopped his head back on the table.

"Are your folks okay?" Eric asked, trying to sound empathetic.

"Yes, Eric. Everyone is just fine." Aaron waited for the sarcasm which usually followed.

"You know I was only kidding earlier, right? As pathetic as it may sound, since Neal died, you guys are all I have. As far as I'm concerned, you're family. I know that sometimes I act like a jerk, but—"

"Stop." Aaron held up a hand. "Don't be silly. Just forget about it. If you can't make a fool of yourself in front of family, where can you? You know I never take you seriously."

"Are you sure?"

"Would you feel better if I just punched you and got it over with?"

"I said I was sorry, not delirious." Eric was happy to have a friend like Aaron.

"I aim to please. Let me know if you change your mind."

"You guys are killing my buzz. Why don't you two just kiss and make up already?" Christopher leaned across the table and knocked over the last bit of Aaron's club soda.

"Sorry, guys, I'm cutting you off." Jennifer handed Aaron a napkin.

"That's fine. It's time for us to bounce anyway." Aaron dropped a tip on the table. He knew all the guys left her pretty good tips, but twenty was all he could afford. But even though he couldn't afford to leave her as much as some of the other guys, she always seemed to appreciate the effort.

"See you later," Jennifer mouthed.

Aaron winked.

"What was that?" Eric demanded.

"What was what?"

"What was that? You can't deny that you guys just had a 'moment.'" Eric wasn't letting this go.

"She was the teaching assistant in my art history class."

"It's a little late for extra credit, wouldn't you say?"

Aaron and Eric helped Christopher to the car.

"I'm sorry that Sarah won't be back in the country in time for graduation." Aaron said with genuine concern.

Eric shrugged. "It couldn't be helped. She really wanted to be here."

"Yeah, so what are you doing after graduation?" Aaron asked. He knew that Eric would be too proud to ask to join anyone else's festivities.

"He's having dinner with me and my folks," Christopher insisted. "There is no way I'm facing Mitch and Laura, sober and alone."

"I guess I'll be eating with Christopher's family," Eric laughed. "Go back to sleep, you moron. Let's just hope you'll be sober enough to join your parents and me."

Chapter Four

As Eric prepared the centrifuge, he glanced at the clock. He still had time to run one last experiment. He wanted to make the day last as long as possible. He was happy about his new job, but he knew that he was going to miss the Newton Center. It had become his second home since graduation. College had taught him science, but it had been the Center that had taught him to be a scientist.

"What are you still doing here, Eric? I thought you were meeting your friends across town to celebrate the new job." Sarah shook her head. Eric had become the son she wished she'd raised, instead of her lazy, spoiled brood at home.

"I was just trying to finish running this test. I hate leaving a huge pile for the next guy. I must have just lost track of time."

"You should know that our job is never finished. There is always going to be just one more test to run. But it's refreshing to have worked with such a dedicated worker. We're really going to miss you." She took the Petri dish from his hand. "Now go; be with your friends. Enjoy your last night in New York. As much as you think you hate big-city life, you are really going to miss it."

"Don't worry; I have time to finish this test and still make it to the bar on time. Besides, Aaron and Christopher are riding together, and Christopher is never on time to anything. His mother swears he was late to his own birth, and he'll be late to his own funeral."

"Which one is Christopher again? The liberal save-the-world wannabe or the legal social climber?" Sarah smiled.

Eric eyed her in mock rebuke.

"I'm just joking with you," Sarah insisted. "I've always liked them. I'm sure they're both lovely boys. I'm just happy you have such good friends."

Eric shrugged and took back the dish.

"Why are you really stalling?"

"I'm not stalling." He turned his attentions back to his test.

"Yes, you are, and I think I know why."

He met her gaze.

"Your friends are going to be just as happy for you as we are, and if they're not, they aren't your friends," Sarah reassured him.

"I don't know. They're both very involved in the church, and I know that their church is against any research involving the use of any of 'God's creatures.' It was their church that organized that protest last month, and we only experiment using nonhuman specimens. I figure if they have problems with the work we're doing here, they're really going to have problems with the stem-cell research being done at Grayson Labs. I really think they may be conflicted about my choice to work there. I just hope that they can put their opinions aside and just be happy for me."

"It's your life. You are the only one to whom you have to justify yourself. I'm sure you don't agree with every decision they've made either. You know where we are, so if things don't go well, just bring your tail back here, and we'll send you off the right way."

"Thanks so much for all you've done."

"You don't have anything to thank me for. You earned that job."

"Yeah, right, and I suppose you had nothing to do with it."

She grinned. "Well, I might have helped a little."

"Thanks, and not just for the job. Thanks for everything."

"I know that you're going to change the world for the better. You'll do amazing things. It was my pleasure to just play a small part in all that you are going to accomplish."

There was so much he wanted to tell her, but he didn't know how. How could he tell her that knowing that she was proud of him meant as much to him as the job itself, or that she'd been more to him than just a mentor—she'd been like a mother. Words were never his strong suit and hugging her would have been completely inappropriate.

Sarah grabbed his hand. She pulled him to her and hugged him. He tried to force back his emotions but then gave way to them. Somehow, he didn't mind being vulnerable in front of her.

"I want you to know that you always have a family and a home here at the Center," she whispered into his ear. When she let go, he held on just a little longer. She smiled. "Now go have some fun, but don't stay out too long. You need your rest for tomorrow, and I wouldn't want you to oversleep."

Eric turned to leave.

"You might need this." She held out his umbrella. "It's raining out."

"Thanks." Eric took the umbrella and reached for the doorknob but then paused, turning toward the smiling woman.

Sarah held out a closed fist.

"I guess I better take those as well." He held out his hand, and Sarah handed him his keys.

Sarah had never seen him so anxious. He was so nervous about telling his friends about the new job. She hoped they didn't let him down. As brilliant a man as he had become, in so many ways he was still just a little boy, wanting to please the people around him.

****

Aaron listened to the news report as he waited for Christopher to finish dressing. "Did you hear about this?"

"What?" Christopher asked.

"Another kid just went missing on the eastside. They say the police think it's the same guy."

"How do they know it's the same guy?"

"I don't know. I'm sure they have ways of telling." Aaron sat on the coffee table to listen to the rest of the news report. He checked his watch. "Christopher! Aren't you ready yet?"

"I'm almost ready." Christopher ran the electric shaver over his face

"You can do that in the car. You usually do."

"I just want to look good tonight, just in case."

"In case of what?"

"Didn't you notice how excited he sounded?"

"And?"

"And this could be it."

"You think he's found someone, don't you?"

"Don't you? What else could it be?" Christopher beamed. He was so excited for his friend. Sure, Eric had dated lots of women, but never for long. Whenever things started going well, he'd get scared and find an excuse to leave.

"No, I don't. I'll tell you what I think. I think he got a promotion."

"What makes you think it's a job?" asked Christopher.

"The only thing that gets Eric this worked up is science. Don't you remember the whole 'science as the one true religion' speech he gave in Sunday school the last time we took him with us to church?"

"Oh, yeah. Sister Emma is still praying for him and placing him on the altar before God every Sunday over that speech." Christopher smiled as he reminisced.

"I think she thinks he's the devil. She even said that she had a vision of his bringing great turmoil to the earth in the name of his god, science."

"I almost forgot about that. That was pretty scary. You know that Sister Emma has a good track record with her visions, and she was so sure."

"Yeah, that was pretty uncomfortable."

Christopher grabbed his jacket. "I'm ready."

"It's about time."

Eric slowed as he approached the gallery. Of all the places in the research center, this had been his favorite. This was where he came to commune with those who had gone before him and to ponder the answers to the meaning of life. He walked reverently pass the portraits of all the many scientists who'd forged the path he now traveled. He might one day return but never to that moment. He knew, as researchers came and went, things would change; he would change, and he wanted to hold on to that moment a while longer.

Eric took a deep breath and stepped out into the night air. It was cool and damp but not at all unpleasant. He took a moment to breathe in the coolness of the night before hailing a cab, but he decided to walk instead. He fell into rhythm with the sounds of the city. He could not believe that he was going to miss the sirens, the horns, even the strange low hum of the neon lights overhead that had annoyed him ever since arriving in Manhattan all those years ago, but there it was.

****

"I can't believe we beat Eric here." Aaron proclaimed their small victory as he scanned the bar.

"I told you we were going to be on time."

"Despite your best efforts."

Christopher's cell phone rang. "Hey, Eric. We've been here half the night. Where are you?" Christopher teased.

"I'm right behind you. I spotted you guys when you walked into the bar." Eric motioned to his friends.

Aaron and Christopher turned to see Eric waving at them from the back of the crowded bar, so they braved the gauntlet of tables set too close together, with people packed into a much-too-small space, as they made their way to the table.

"Hey, guys. I can't believe you're on time."

"We had to find out more about this spectacular news." Aaron grabbed a seat.

"Wait. Let me guess. Now, Aaron says it's a promotion, but I'm standing behind my initial impression. I'm saying that's it's a girl—no, no, no, wait: *the* girl."

"So what is it? What's the huge announcement? Are we looking at a new wife or a new life?" Aaron was certain that only a new job could make Eric this happy.

"Hold that thought." Eric paused as their round of drinks arrived.

Aaron started to protest. "I'll just have—"

"I know, Aaron. Don't worry; it's only club soda, with lemon."

"Thanks."

The men all raised their glasses.

"I'd like you guys to help me toast my new job." Eric was excited to share his news with his best friends.

"I told you. Wait. Did you mean new promotion or new job?"

"It's actually a new job. I'm leaving in the morning."

"What do you mean, leaving? How can you be moving in the morning? How long have you known? When did you pack?" Christopher couldn't believe what he was hearing.

"I'm not leaving tomorrow for good. They just want me to report for a week, and then I'll be back to pack up the apartment. They're actually paying for me to relocate."

"I thought you loved your job. I didn't even know you were looking. So where is it?" Aaron wanted to show his support. He knew how important their approval was to Eric, and it was obvious that this job meant a lot to him.

"This is a huge promotion. It's one of the most cutting-edge facilities in the country. There were hundreds of applicants, but they chose me."

"Okay. That sounds great, but where is it?" Christopher asked.

"It's at Grayson Labs in Colorado."

"Grayson Labs?" Aaron could not believe what he was hearing. He knew that Eric was ambitious, but he could not believe that even Eric would consider working for a lab known for its human-rights violations and questionable ethics.

"They're doing some of the most cutting-edge work in the world. It's a real honor to have been chosen." Eric was so full of pride that he had not detected the aversion in Aaron's voice.

"Wow! Have you ever even been to Colorado?" Christopher seemed still in shock by the news.

"No, but I couldn't care less about where I live. The important thing is that I'll be working at one of the most progressive research labs in the world."

Aaron wanted to say something positive, but he could not think of anything that would not sound phony. He was afraid that his disgust would be apparent, even in the tone of his voice, so he kept silent.

Eric confronted Aaron. "Your silence speaks volumes, so you might as well just say what we know you're thinking."

"Are you aware that they've been fined by the government more than a half dozen times for performing questionable research and that they're on the top of the watch lists of pro-life, PETA, and human rights groups?"

"Can we not do the liberal crap for one night? Of course not; what was I thinking? Silly me to think you could just put your ideals aside for one moment and just be happy for me."

"I am happy for you."

"Then what is your problem?"

"I don't have a problem with you. I'm happy for you. I know how much this must mean to you." Aaron tried to sound supportive.

"Right, because you know me so well."

"So when do we get to visit? I hear Colorado has great rafting and gorgeous women," Christopher said, trying unsuccessfully to change the topic.

"I guess I was crazy to expect you to be happy for me. How about you, Christopher? Do you have a problem with my new job?"

"I'm proud of what you've accomplished. It sounds like the competition was ferocious." Christopher patted Eric on the back, but Eric pulled away.

"Spoken like a true politician. Mitch would be so proud of you."

"Come on, Eric, that's not fair. We can be happy for you without supporting the type of research being performed at the lab. They don't have to be exclusive of each other," Christopher protested.

"You mean the type of work I'll be doing at the lab."

"I'm sorry I even said anything. It just took me by surprise. We're your best friends. We're always going to believe in you," Aaron insisted.

"I thought Christopher was going to be the politician. How can you believe in me, and not believe in what I do." Eric stood up to leave. He threw several twenties on the table. "I've got this round of drinks."

"Don't leave like this," Christopher pleaded. He followed Eric out to the street. "This is silly. It's just a misunderstanding."

"You know what's ironic? My friends at the lab offered to take me out to celebrate, but I told them I had plans with my buddies." Eric laughed bitterly as he hailed a cab. "I thought leaving was going to be hard. Thank you for making this so easy."

Christopher returned to the bar.

"I'm sorry. I didn't mean to make him feel badly. I just wanted to—" Aaron tried to explain.

"I know, but you can't say everything that enters your mind. Sometimes it's best to just pray about a situation and let God sort things out. If he doesn't intervene, then what right do we have to stop him? Don't worry. He'll be fine. We should just give him a few days." Christopher tried to reassure Aaron, but he had never seen Eric so angry. He only hoped Eric would calm down after he had had an opportunity to think things over. He knew Aaron had meant well, but sometimes he was a little too zealous.

Aaron could not have felt guiltier for ruining Eric's big night. "We don't have a few days. He's leaving tomorrow."

"Yes, but he'll be back in a week. We'll hook up with him later. It'll be fine." Christopher insisted. He hoped things would be that easy to repair.

As Sarah approached the parking garage, she saw Eric standing near her car. She had hoped things would go well, but the look on Eric face reflected just the opposite. She held out her hands to him as she approached.

"What are you doing back so soon? When I said not to stay out too late, I didn't mean for you to cut your night this short."

Eric was silent. He didn't have to say anything.

Those idiots, she thought. "Let's grab a drink before I take you home."

Eric nodded and got into the front seat of her car.

Chapter Five

Eric arrived an hour early for his meeting. He always liked to allow extra time to acclimate himself to new situations. This was his first day at Grayson Labs, and he wanted to make a great impression; being late was not an option. He had set three alarm clocks to ensure that he did not oversleep, but all his added precautions had proven unnecessary. He was so excited that he was already dressed a half-hour before he was supposed to be awake.

He counted it a privilege to be one of the two scientists offered a position that year at what was, without a doubt, the most prestigious stem-cell research center in the United States, if not the world. Since the lab always promoted from within, and employee turnover was uncommonly low, openings were rare. Grayson was known the world over for pressing the international legal envelope, and it had the successful results to show for it.

Eric fully expected this to be the beginning of an illustrious career. He planned to approach this new challenge the way he approached every other challenge in his life; he would take a strategic, if not defensive, approach. He would arrive earlier than everyone else and leave later. He would make the right connections, and—most important—he would stay focused on his goal by blocking out any and all distractions.

As Eric pulled into his parking space, he saw a young woman reaching for something under her car. She had lifted her skirt slightly to allow herself to maneuver into the precarious position. He noticed the outline of her slender legs under the tightly drawn skirt and the way her long hair almost touched the ground as she reached farther under the car. He noticed everything, except the post in front of his car—that is, until he hit it.

The loud noise startled the woman. She ran to see if Eric was okay. Eric couldn't believe his misfortune. He'd been there less than fifteen minutes, and he'd already managed to damage private property and embarrass himself in front of the most beautiful woman he had ever seen.

"Are you all right?" she asked.

"I'm fine. I think the post and my pride were the only casualties of my absent-minded moment."

"It doesn't look too bad. I think if you back your car away from the post, no one will even notice."

Eric backed the car several inches away from the post before getting out of his car to assess the damages. It was a rental, and he was glad that he had opted for the extra insurance.

The woman extended her hand. "Hi. I'm Sharay."

"I'm Eric."

"It is nice to meet you, Eric. I don't think I've seen you around the lab before. Is this your first day?"

"Yes, but unfortunately, I had hoped to make a better first impression."

"Don't you hate first days? They never seem to go the way you plan."

"Yeah. I know what you mean."

She winked at him. "Don't worry. My lips are sealed."

Eric blushed. "Thanks."

"No problem. It'll be our little secret."

"Well, then, I insist that you at least allow me to take you to dinner to show you my appreciation."

"You mean, like a bribe?" she asked.

"Sure, if you're not opposed to bribes." Eric was usually more direct, but he was enjoying the cat-and-mouse game.

"I love them, especially ones that end in flowers."

"I think that can be arranged."

She smiled as she tucked a loose strand of hair behind her ear.

"Are you trying to drive me crazy?" Eric teased.

"Only if it's working."

"I think it's safe to say that it's working." Eric smiled. He was delighted to have met someone with such a great sense of humor. He hadn't expected to make a friend so quickly; it had been enough for him to just be there. He was sure it was going to be a great day.

"Follow me," Sharay instructed him. "I'll show you were the lab is. We wouldn't want you to be late on your first day."

"Sassy and coy. I guess I hit the jackpot."

"Only if you play your cards right."

****

As Christopher sat across from his father, listening to him go on and on about duty and honor, he waited for the real reason that Mitch had invited him to lunch.

"How's work?" Mitch asked.

"Great. I just got assigned as the lead council on a high-profile case the firm just inherited. I can't say too much yet, but this could be huge. All the partners are preoccupied with ongoing cases of their own, so they had to give it to an associate. They chose me over Morgan, and he has seniority."

"That's a great sign."

"I think so," Christopher agreed.

"How is Sandy?"

There it was—the real reason his father had invited him to lunch. It couldn't have been just to be supportive. It always had to be about some imagined shortcoming. Either he drank too much or talked too loudly. His friends were too poor or too frivolous. This time, it was his romantic life. Christopher sighed. "Her name is Sasha, but then I'm sure you know that already."

"Fine; how is Sasha?"

"She's fine."

"How do the partners feel about your relationship with one of their secretaries?"

"I wouldn't know. Besides, we're only dating."

"I'll guarantee you that Morgan isn't dating a secretary."

"What does whom I decide to date have to do with anything?" Christopher wanted to know.

"It shows judgment. One mistake can derail a career forever."

"Who are we talking about? Me or you?"

"This has nothing to do with our family," Mitch growled. "You know how I feel about you and your mother."

"Do I?" What Christopher did know was that his father had always blamed his mother for stalling his political career.

"I love your mother very much, but my relationship with her—"

"Enough! I will not have this conversation." Christopher rose to leave.

Mitch grabbed Christopher's sleeve and pulled him back into the seat. "Sit down, and lower your voice. I'm not blaming your mother. I'm not disappointed with my life, but I have wondered what I could have done differently."

Years ago, Christopher's father had been married to a political insider. Theirs had been more of a merging of ambitions than a union of love, but for years, that had been enough. As both their careers skyrocketed, it was apparent that their marriage served both of their goals. Together, they seemed unstoppable.

Mitch's career had been the most important thing in his life—until he met Laura. She was the personal secretary his firm had hired to assist him. The more time they spent together, the more time he wanted to spend with her. He found himself inventing reasons to work late, so that they could spend more time together. He convinced himself that his intentions were harmless, until the night they took their innocent flirtations to the next level. He had known what he was risking. Not only would his career be adversely affected, but he and his wife were friends, and he hadn't wanted to hurt her.

When Laura became pregnant, the information was leaked to the media. Affairs were not uncommon among the political elite and would have been easily overlooked; a pregnancy, however, made that impossible. As pro-life conservatives, an abortion was never an option, so Mitch's wife had opted for a divorce over the humiliation of helping her husband to raise his mistress's child. Though openly she supported him through the turmoil, privately, they both knew that their marriage was over. As soon as the scandal subsided, she discreetly sought a divorce, and with her went most of Mitch's political prospects and all of her family's money.

"I get it. My mother destroyed your career, and I dealt your marriage a final death blow." Christopher hailed a waiter and ordered a vodka martini.

Mitch canceled the order. "What are you doing? You can't go back to your office smelling like booze this early in the afternoon."

Christopher rolled his eyes.

"Don't be so sensitive. I'm not sorry I married your mother; she gave me you, and although I may not say it enough, I'm proud to be your father."

Christopher was shocked. These were sentiments Mitch rarely—if ever—expressed.

"I know that I'm a lousy husband and an even worse father," Mitch went on.

"Don't say that. That's not fair."

"No, but it's accurate. I've allowed your mother to shoulder the burden of my failed career, when I was the one who relentlessly pursued her. You're an amazing son. I tell all my friends how lucky I am, but when it comes time to tell you how I feel, my words fail me, and I just make matters worse. You would think that someone who makes his living by always saying the right thing would be better at this." Mitch motioned for the waiter and ordered a drink.

"I thought you said we shouldn't return to the office smelling like booze," Christopher reminded his father.

"I'm not going back to the office. I'm taking a recommended leave of absence. I've been a little preoccupied with some health concerns and have allowed some of my work duties to slip."

"What health concerns? Is it serious?" Christopher's voice cracked.

"Don't worry. The doctor says if I take things easy, I should be around for quite some time. I have to be there to see you take Washington by storm."

"Do you really believe I can do this?"

"I know you can. You are your father's son." Mitch finished his drink. "I fear you may even be a little too much like me, if you know what I mean."

"All right, I'll end it tonight. But she's not what you think. She's a great girl."

"I'm sure she is, but she's not the right girl for your future."

Christopher nodded.

Mitch changed the topic. "Tell me about this case of yours."

****

Neal hung up the phone and lay across the couch. His talk with Sharay's sister, Angela, had gone remarkably well. She had been more than happy to give him candid information concerning Sharay. He actually found himself looking forward to the opportunity to see her again. He made plans with Angela under the pretense of continuing their discussion of Sharay and his brother. Though he had slightly exaggerated his concerns when speaking to her, it was true that his thoughts were rarely far from Eric. Not being able to contact him was difficult, but watching him achieve success made things a little easier.

"So how does Eric like his new job?" Balile asked.

"He loves it, and he's met someone."

"Really? That was fast." Balile tried to sound surprised.

"Her name is Sharay, as I'm sure you and the Triad already know. She works in his department. He may have finally met the first girl in his life who truly gets him."

"Is that wise at this time?" Balile pressed. "Just as he was selected years ago as the father of our movement, so was its mother.

"I know what you are thinking, and I won't interfere, at least not until I have to. He's been through so much, and it's enough for me that he is happy. Is that too much to ask for?"

"Have you at least had her investigated?" Balile asked.

"Of course I did, and I plan to interview the sister, Angela, again later. I've submitted a report to the Triad, detailing all of this. I know and they know that she doesn't fit the profile, but I say, so what? Maybe she's not 'the

One,' but for the time being, Eric is happy for a change, which in my book definitely makes her the right one for now."

Balile heard the aggravation in Neal's voice, so he decided to back off. Maybe Neal was right. Maybe Eric's relationship with Sharay was good for him … but eventually, Sharay would have to be removed from the equation.

****

Eric looked across the table. He enjoyed watching Sharay eat. He loved the way she savored each bite as if it were the most delectable morsel she'd ever tasted. As he watched her, he was reminded of their first date. Though it had been months ago, he remembered it as if it were yesterday. They had gone out for ice cream, and she had worn a short red dress that accented her every curve. He had spent the entire night watching her longingly. With each spoonful of ice cream she ate, she had taken his breath away. He watched as her moist tongue traced the outline of her upper lip. It drove him crazy, and she seemed to love it.

Sharay smiled as she became aware of Eric's gaze. She liked the way he watched her when he thought she wasn't aware. She tilted her head slightly as she brushed a stray strand of hair out of her face. *Take that*, she thought.

"I love to watch you eat."

"I'm happy that my eating brings you so much pleasure." She enjoyed teasing him.

He blushed. "I can't believe I said that out loud."

"Don't worry. Your secret is safe with me."

"Yes, you've already proven you can keep a secret."

"So, are you going to tell me what the special occasion is?" she pressed.

"Does it have to be a special occasion for me to take out the woman that I love?"

Sharay's smile was replaced by shock. He just used the "L" word.

Eric reached into his pocket and pulled out a small box. He placed it on the table in front of Sharay. She gasped. She adored him, but she wasn't sure that they were ready for a permanent commitment. Things were going so well. She didn't want to spoil things by moving too quickly.

"Okay, you're right," Eric admitted. "I did ask you here for a special reason. We've been seeing each other for about four months now, and I can honestly say that I've never felt this way about anyone before. Sharay, will you move in with me?" Eric opened the box, revealing a copy of his apartment key.

Sharay was instantly flooded with both relief and elation. "Yes! Yes!" she screamed and hugged him tightly.

"You should have seen your face when I pulled out the box."

"You did that on purpose? You can be such a jerk." She playfully punched him. "What if I had wanted you to give me a ring? What if I had been disappointed when you didn't ask me to marry you?"

"There was no chance of that."

"Why would you say that?" Though she wasn't ready for marriage yet either, she needed to know that he hadn't ruled it out for the future.

"You love your freedom as much as I love mine. Neither of us is ready to settle down. That's why we get along so well."

"What if I decide one day that I want you all to myself?"

"We can cross that mine field when we come to it." Eric raised his glass. "Here's to living life on our terms."

****

Neal waited for an hour in the rain before his contact finally arrived. The man handed him a dossier. Neal reluctantly accepted the envelope, and returned to his car to read it.

As Neal flipped through the pages, tears began to sting the corners of his eyes. Hadn't his family paid enough for the call on their lives? Hadn't Eric been through enough?

"Bad news?" Angela asked.

"The Triad has decided that it is time to move forward."

"And that's a bad thing, why?"

"According to prophesy, the holy child must walk in both camps," Neal tried to explain.

"What does that mean?"

"His mother must be a Christian, and as we both know, Sharay is not."

"She never was, so what has changed?"

"Everything, and now it is up to me to set things right."

"How do you plan to do that? Eric loves Sharay."

"When Sharay visits her gynecologist in a week, she's going to leave with a gift she didn't expect."

"I don't understand."

"Eric has lost everyone he's ever allowed himself to get close to, so now he's afraid of a commitment. Once again, I have to use the fears that I helped create against him. What a great brother I am."

"Gods always require the most from their most beloved subjects. It's true in Christianity, and it's true with the master. He will reward our blind faith and unwavering obedience. He never takes more than he gives. He is a righteous father. Isn't that what you have been teaching me?" Angela tried to console him.

Neal forced himself to smile. She was right. No one said this would be easy. Nothing worth having ever was. Balile was right, too. Neal should never have let things go this far; now, his brother was going to have to pay the price. Nothing good had come from allowing Eric and Sharay to continue their relationship—except for his meeting Angela.

"So where are they sending him?" she asked.

He handed Angela the dossier and started the car. "Back to New York."

Chapter Six

Sharay eyed her lunch. She couldn't bring herself to take a bite. She knew she had to tell him eventually, but somehow, the words wouldn't form on her tongue. She poked at her salad.

"Okay." Eric put down his fork.

"Okay?" Sharay looked up.

"Yes, tell me. I know you have something to tell me. You haven't eaten a bite. How bad can it be?"

"I'm pregnant." There, she had said it.

Eric's eyes turned cold. "What do you plan to do?"

"Don't you mean *we*?" she asked, her voice cracking.

"Oh, I'm sorry. Do I get a vote?" Eric's sarcasm forced its way to the surface. She eyed him angrily. "You know how I feel about becoming a father. I've never hidden that from you. I've told you about my awful childhood. I'm not willing to risk putting my own child through that kind of hell unless I'm sure that I'm ready. We both agreed that we weren't ready."

"Things change."

"Not everything. Not for me."

"Do you think this is what I wanted?" Sharay demanded.

"I don't know what you want anymore. You have to do what you have to do."

"I didn't do this on my own."

"Yes, but you get to decide what happens on your own. You get to make all the decisions, decisions that will affect both of our lives forever."

"Is that all you have to say?" She couldn't believe how angry he was. She expected him to be upset, but not hostile, not cruel.

"Don't look at me that way. What do you want me to say? It's obvious that you've made your decision. Why else would you be telling me here in our restaurant?"

"I wanted your input. Like you said, this affects both of our lives. I wanted us to talk to each other about this."

"I've already done all the talking I plan to do. My feelings haven't changed, even if yours have. The ball's in your court. Do you plan to keep it?"

"I don't know."

"Then let me know when you decide." Eric threw his napkin on the table and rose to leave.

"Please!" she pleaded.

"I'll see you at the lab." He kissed her forehead before leaving. "Think hard about this."

On the way home, Sharay took a walk in the park to clear her head. Could she raise this child on her own? Did she want to?

Growing up, she hadn't been like other little girls. She and her sister, Angela, had never played with dolls or dreamed of becoming mothers, but she couldn't ignore the fact that things had changed. Finding out that she was pregnant had had more of an effect on her than she would have expected. For the first time in her life, she could imagine being a mother.

She tried to think rationally about her situation and to keep her emotions out of it, but images of holding her child made this impossible. She touched her stomach. What proof did she have that Eric would ever be ready for fatherhood, or that she'd ever get another chance at motherhood? She decided that she would keep her baby. She picked up her cell phone to call Eric. She knew she had to do it quickly, before she lost her nerve.

Eric was noticeably shaken when he returned to the office. He had not intended to be so hurtful but had panicked when Sharay told him that she was pregnant. He knew that she could never fully appreciate the baggage he carried, nor should she be expected to understand, but he wished he would have at least made an attempt to explain. He owed her that.

Eric didn't know what to do, but he did know that he didn't want to lose Sharay. She was the first woman he'd dated for more than a few weeks, and he had really begun to care for her. He picked up the receiver to call her, but hung up the phone after dialing only the first few numbers. What did he want to tell her? What could he say? Instead, he called Sarah. "I don't want to push her away," he moaned. "Maybe keeping the baby wouldn't be the end of the world."

"Let me ask you—do you want this child? Are you ready for fatherhood?" Sarah was careful not to push too hard.

"I don't know."

"Nor do I, but I can tell you that an unwanted child can be a cruse. Think hard before you buckle under pressure. You can't change your mind if things don't work. You care about her now, but can you say for sure how you'll feel ten years from now?"

"How can I know that?" Eric felt even more conflicted.

"Exactly. You'll be this child's father forever, and whether or not you and Sharay stay together, you'll be linked to Sharay for the rest of your life as well."

"You think keeping it would be a mistake?"

"I think you both need time to know where your relationship is heading. If you're meant to be, there will be plenty of time for all the children in the world."

One the technicians interrupted. "I'm sorry, Eric, you have another call."

"I have to run," Eric explained to Sarah. "I have another call."

"Call me back if you need to talk."

"Hello."

"It's me." Sharay tried to keep her voice from cracking.

"I'm so sorry. I shouldn't have acted like such a bully; it just took me off guard. I mean, we were so careful. I know it's your body and your decision. You know I really care for you, and I really want you in my future; but this is not the right time for me. I'm just not ready for this kind of commitment." He chose his words carefully.

"What do you call living together, if not a commitment?" Sharay remained firm in her resolve to keep the child. He was right about one thing. It was her decision, and whatever she decided, she would have to live with it forever.

"Look, you know what kind of childhood my brother and I had. I know it sounds like an excuse, but I just want to do it right when the time comes. I don't want to make any mistakes. I know what I'm asking you is huge. I just need more time, and you alone have the power to buy us that time. We can have as many babies as you want when the time is right. We can be just like the other breeders." They both laughed. "I know you have to do what you feel is right, but I'm begging you to consider what's best for all of us."

Sharay felt her resolve wavering. How could she risk destroying everything that they had created? It wasn't fair to them—or to the child. What right did she have to bring an unwanted child into the world? Maybe Eric would come around, but maybe he wouldn't. What if he never wanted their child and resented her for forcing him to do something he wasn't ready to do? That would be the worst thing for everyone, including the baby.

"Okay," she agreed.

"Okay? You'll do it."

"I said I would. Let's just do this and get it over." She wiped away a tear.

"Right now?"

"Let's do it before I change my mind."

"I'll be right there."

****

Christopher rushed across town to meet Aaron. They had standing reservations every Friday at a local eatery around the corner from the courthouse. Since both had become so busy, this gave them the opportunity to keep up with each other's lives. As usual, Christopher was running a little late.

"She's a reporter," Christopher warned Aaron.

"So what?"

"She's ambitious."

"So are you. That doesn't make you a bad guy."

"That depends on who you ask. So you really like this girl, huh?" Christopher shook his head in bewilderment. He couldn't imagine what Aaron could possibly see in her.

"I know she's a little rough around the edges, but once you get to know her, she's great." Aaron didn't care about her rough edges; he just enjoyed her company.

"You don't seem to have a whole lot in common."

"How would you know? You've barely said two words to her."

"I just never would have picked her for you." Christopher knew the type. He wished Aaron could see her for who she really was.

"Well, I guess I'm lucky you're not the one doing the picking," Aaron protested.

"We'll see how glad you are after you've been together a few months."

"Yes, we will."

"Are you serious?" Christopher could not believe that Aaron was actually considering pursuing a relationship with Katrina. She was easily one of the most self-absorbed people imaginable.

"I'm just saying that maybe I'm ready for a stable relationship," Aaron explained.

"Say it ain't so, bro. Who'll be my wing man if you settle down?"

"Maybe you should consider giving monogamy a chance." Aaron dismissed Christopher's warning. He wasn't about to take relationship advice from the biggest playboy he knew.

"What? Deprive all the sweeties of spending time with me?" Christopher scoffed. "Now I know you've lost your mind. Look, I'm not saying don't settle down; I'm just saying …"

"What *are* you saying?"

"You know I've always been supportive."

Aaron shook his head. "No, you haven't."

"I backed you up, even when you decided to leave graduate school your final year to enter seminary"

"I seem to remember your being one of my biggest critics."

"What did I know?" Christopher laughed. "I did, however, come around, and now I'm one of you biggest supporters."

"Yes, you are, but now that I'm a minister, I have responsibilities. It's time for me to put away childish things. It's time to start thinking about settling down with the right woman."

"So, you think Katrina Callahan's the one?"

"It's just a date."

"A fifth date."

"Okay. It's a fifth date."

****

Across town, the police scoured the woods surrounding the park where nine-year-old Marcus Allen was last seen. Though only a few hours had passed, experience told the investigating officers that this was the work of their serial abductor, and they did not expect to find any evidence that would lead to the safe return of the young child.

The lead officer on the case was Officer Callahan. He'd served on the force many years, but he'd never seen anything like these cases. He examined the ritualistically mutilated animal remains discovered that morning.

"Could it be a copycat?" asked Callahan's partner. He had just been transferred to Callahan's unit, and so he knew few of the facts surrounding the high-profile case.

"I don't see how it could be. Everything is exactly the same, right down to the carvings. We never divulge the symbols carved into any of the animals, and these markings are a spot-on match."

"How many does this make?"

"There have been eight boys within the last six years in Manhattan alone. There have been several other similar disappearances other places, but the slight deviations make it impossible to rule out a different killer," Callahan explained.

"You mean different as in another group?"

"We believe it's the same group, just a different member, but we can't know for sure."

"May I quote you on that?" The two officers turned to see Callahan's sister, Katrina, who was a reporter for the *Star*.

"This story is a little out of your league, wouldn't you say?" Callahan asked.

"I don't plan to cover gallery openings for the rest of my life."

The officer in charge of keeping the media at bay stepped up and said, "I'm sorry, sir. She said it was a family emergency. I asked her to wait while I came to get you."

Callahan nodded. "It's all right. I'll handle this." He grabbed Katrina by the arm and led her away from the crime scene.

"What can you tell me?" Katrina pressed.

"Pay your dues, and stop trying to use me to get you what hard work should." He kept a tight grip on her arm as he escorted her back to the press line. "Keep everyone out," he ordered the officer in charge of controlling the crowd.

"Why are you searching this side of the park?" Katrina called to him as he walked away. "I thought the boy went missing from the west side."

Callahan's partner pretended not to notice Callahan's embarrassment. "I didn't know you had a sister."

"Neither do I—until I have a big case."

****

Sharay found the abortion clinic deceptively warm. All the women could have just as easily been waiting to have their hair and nails done.

"Sharay Adams!" the nurse called. Eric squeezed her hand. It startled her. She had almost forgotten he was there.

"It's going to be fine," he reassured her.

"Yes, I know." She forced a smile.

Eric rose to accompany her.

"I'm sorry, you can't go with her," the nurse said, "but we're going to take good care of her. Don't worry."

Eric slowly released her hand. He knew that they were making the best decision, but he also knew that this was not what Sharay wanted. He hoped she would not regret it. He hoped their relationship would survive. She looked back at him one last time as the nurse led her to a room.

"Put this on, and wait here," the nurse instructed as she handed Sharay a medical gown. "The doctor will be with you shortly."

Sharay slowly undressed. She looked around the small room filled with pictures of beautiful flowers and delightful sunrises on amazing sand-covered beaches. She imagined Eric lying with her on the tranquil shores of some faraway beach, maybe even the one in the picture.

"Hello, I'm Dr. Vargus." His voice startled her. Sharay had been so lost in thought, that she hadn't heard him come in. "Let me get you to relax on the table."

She could not relax. The table was cold and felt awkward. She tried to readjust her position, but nothing seemed to help. She closed her eyes and tried to wish it all away. She was surprised to hear a baby crying in the next room.

After the abortion, she was at once struck by the loss. She tried to be brave, but she could not stop the flow of tears.

The nurse handed Sharay a tissue. "Don't worry, honey. It's not uncommon to be a little emotional afterwards. You'll be just fine. The procedure went well, and you're still so young. You have plenty of time."

Sharay took several deep breaths. Somehow, the pictures were not quite so beautiful anymore. The flowers seemed dull and the beaches lonely. She inquired about the crying child in the next room.

"Oh, no, sweetie, we never allow babies in the back," the nurse reassured her, "You know, for obvious reasons. Maybe you just heard the machines."

****

Aaron left the church early. He didn't want to be late picking up his date, Katrina. Though art-gallery showings were not his favorite pastime, they were frequented by some of New York's finest, and he was flattered that she had thought enough of him to ask him to accompany her.

Aaron escorted Katrina into the gallery. He understood that she was working, and they planned to go out to dinner afterwards, so he watched as she mingled with the other guests.

"I really appreciate this. I know you hate these types of events. I hate these things, too, but I have to pay my dues if I'm ever going to have my own column. I just wish they'd assign me to cover someone I like," she complained.

"I'm having a delightful evening, and I am enjoying the company."

"You're such a bad liar, but thanks anyway."

"Don't mention it." He kissed her on the check. "Don't worry about me. I can keep myself occupied. I'll just look around the gallery by myself. I happen to think the artist has a wonderful eye."

Before he could ask her the artist's name, Katrina was off again. Aaron hung back as he watched her work the room. This really wasn't his scene, but he did enjoy spending time with her.

"You look a million miles away." A voice from behind him interrupted his train of thought.

He recognized the voice, but he didn't dare turn around, for fear he'd only imagined that she was there. Instead, he just smiled. "So, when did you get back in town?"

"About a year ago."

"You didn't look me up, like you promised."

"Sorry about that, but I figured a man like you wouldn't wait that long for me."

Aaron turned to face her. The moment their eyes met, he knew that they still had unfinished business.

"Aaron!" Katrina called to him as she approached from across the room." She took his hand possessively. "You have to introduce me to your friend."

"Of course, let me introduce you. Jennifer, this is my date, Katrina Callahan; Katrina, this is my good friend Jennifer Shaw. Jennifer and I attended college together." Aaron left out the part about their having dated for over a year.

"Ms. Shaw, this is an honor." Katrina pushed passed Aaron. "You should have told me that you knew the artist, Aaron," she scolded. "I'm sorry that I didn't recognize you Ms. Shaw."

"No, don't mention it. I'm sort of incognito tonight. I get a better idea of how people truly feel about my work."

"Well, I'm here for my paper, and I would love the opportunity to interview you for our art section. I just adore your work. You have such an amazing perspective."

Aaron eyed Katrina in disgust as she lied right in front of him. He wasn't sure if she'd forgotten their earlier conversation concerning her true feeling regarding Jennifer's work, or if she just didn't care and was counting on him to keep his mouth shut. Either way, he found her hypocrisy more than a little difficult to take. Maybe Christopher was right. How could he ever trust anyone who could lie so easily and so well? He almost believed her himself.

"How do you feel about my work?" Jennifer asked Aaron.

"I didn't know this was your work."

"You look surprised."

"The only thing that has taken me by surprise is seeing you after all these years. I'm not, however, surprised that you have become famous. I've always said that you were one of the most creative people I knew."

She blushed and handed him and Katrina a business card. "I really must continue to make my way around the room, but we should catch up." She hugged Aaron. "Please call me, Ms. Callahan, so we can discuss that interview."

Aaron watched as Jennifer walked out of sight, determined that it would not be for the last time.

"You have to keep my secret," Katrina whispered into his ear. "I don't have to like her work to realize how important this interview is for my career." She rushed off to call her editor about her interview with one of New York's most elusive, yet popular rising new artists.

****

Sharay awoke feeling sore. She glanced at the alarm clock; she was late. She tried to get out of the bed but was suddenly gripped by pain. She remembered what she had done. She felt so empty, so alone, so cold. She pulled the blanket tighter, but it offered little warmth.

She had been so certain that she was doing the right thing when she had agreed to the procedure, but now she was not so sure. It was too late to second-guess herself now. She touched her stomach.

"Are you all right?" Eric asked as he entered, caring a tray. "I fixed your breakfast. You need to eat something."

"I'm not hungry. Besides, it's late. You let me oversleep."

"I called the lab. I told them you weren't feeling well."

"That's a delicate way of putting it."

"I don't think they need to know our private business, do you?"

"Whatever you say."

"We did the right thing," Eric reassured her.

"We didn't do it. I did it."

"Okay, you did the right thing. It wasn't the right time for us to become parents."

"That's so funny, because I don't remember your asking me whether I was ready to be a parent or not. I seem to distinctly remember your saying that *you* were not ready to become a parent. I really don't think that I factored into the equation. Do you?"

"What do you want me to say? Do you want me to say I'll make it up to you? I know that you did this for me, and I'll never forget your sacrifice. I just know that this was not the right time for me, but I promise that we'll have other children."

"I don't want you to say anything. I'm not angry. Please, just leave me alone for a while." The truth was that she didn't blame him at all. He hadn't changed his mind, she had. If she had wanted the child, she should have taken a stand. The real difference was that he was willing to fight for his convictions, and she had caved. She only had herself to blame.

"I'm sorry about the baby. I know that you're disappointed." Eric tried to sound sympathetic, but all he really felt was grateful; grateful to still have options; grateful for his freedom; and grateful not to have been forced into fatherhood.

"I've got to go to work. I told them you were sick, not me. I don't think they'll buy both of our being out sick at the same time."

"I understand. I'll be fine."

"We'll do something when I get home." He tried to sound sensitive.

"I'm fine. Just go."

"Sure?"

"I'm fine. I'll be here when you get back."

"Don't worry. It's all over. We never have to speak of this ever again." He kissed her forehead. "I promise."

"I'm just going back to bed." Sharay tried to blink away the tears welling up in the corner of her eyes, but all she managed to do was to dislodge one which raced down her cheek and came to rest on her silk pajamas. She hoped he hadn't noticed. She kissed his cheek.

"I love you," Eric called back to her as he walked down the stairs.

"I know." Sharay closed the door. She sunk to the floor as she cried for the child she would never know. She couldn't help but wonder if it would have been a son or daughter. She'd never get the chance to hold this child or hear it call her Mommy.

She knew that he was lying about having other children, but he need not have made the effort. What she couldn't explain to him was that no other child could replace the one she'd given up for them, and that she could never feel right about being a mother again. They had forfeited their right to be parents.

****

As Marcus Allen lay in a corner of the dark room, curled in a ball, he heard the voices from behind the wall. He sobbed, but there were no tears left in his badly beaten, dehydrated body. He heard the door open, and he curled up tighter. He wanted his mommy and daddy to come get him, but they never did.

Chapter Seven

As Christopher raised his glass to toast the new couple, he felt a slight tug on his jacket. Aaron had warned him to "keep it clean." Everyone laughed. They were all familiar with Christopher's brazen sense of humor.

"I'd like to be first in line to welcome the lovely, the talented, the newly named artist of the year, Mrs. Jennifer Shaw-Drake, to our incredibly dysfunctional family. I knew she was something special the first time she put me in my place after making a fool of myself on graduation night. All jokes aside, to Aaron and Jennifer, may you always remember to treasure each other, and do the little things that over time add up to mean so much. Congratulations!" He hugged Aaron and kissed Jennifer on her cheek.

"Hear! Hear!" the other guests chimed their approval.

Aaron escorted Jennifer to the dance floor for their first dance as husband and wife. He never imagined, all those years ago, that he'd be blessed enough to share the rest of his life with her. He planned to take Christopher's advice and treat each moment they shared together as a moment to be treasured. He pulled her closer as they slow-danced to their favorite song, "Sweet Love."

"Thank you for inviting me to your friends' wedding," Christopher's new campaign manger, Tracy, thanked him.

"Thank you for coming. Like you said, now that I'm running for office, I have to be mindful of the company I keep." He handed her a drink.

As the election drew closer, Christopher became more and more anxious. He wasn't sure what concerned him most—losing or winning—but it felt good to have Tracy with him. "You seem so sure I'm going to win."

"I wish you could see yourself the way we all see you."

"I just hope I don't let you all down."

"Never. Win or lose, you've made a difference." She smiled reassuringly and gently stroked his hand.

He loved it when she touched him. Somehow, it always made him feel that things were not as bad as they appeared. "I've been thinking," he began.

"Should I alert the media?"

"Funny. So you like the classics?"

"They never get old."

Christopher couldn't believe how nervous she made him. "I've been thinking that maybe we could have dinner sometime."

"Dinner?"

"Yes, you know, where we both order food and sit down to eat it together."

"Now who likes the classics?"

"I thought you might appreciate my attempt at humor."

"I'll tell you what; let's just get you elected first."

"I'm going to hold you to that." He smiled.

****

Eric was concerned when their boss, Colten Prescott, asked Sharay to remain late at the lab. Since the unexpected death of the lab's research head, the staff had been putting its best foot forward, each one hoping to be chosen as the new head of research, but Prescott had not made it a secret that he had narrowed his selection between his two best researchers: Eric and Sharay.

Eric checked his watch; it was after midnight. He heard the key turning in the lock and met her at the door. "Where have you been?" he demanded.

Sharay hung up her coat and pushed past him as she made her way to the kitchen.

"Don't I deserve an explanation?" he went on.

"I'm sorry. I thought the question was rhetorical since you know exactly where I was." She fixed herself a sandwich.

"Tell me you didn't sleep with him."

"Okay. I didn't sleep with him."

"Liar! You always eat after sex."

"I also eat when I'm hungry." She continued to eat her sandwich.

He rolled his eyes at her.

"You've made up your mind. Why are you asking me?"

"Did you want the promotion that badly?"

"That must be it." She shot him an angry gaze.

"I can't believe you'd do this to me."

"Yet here you are, accusing me."

"Then you're denying it?"

"Not that I'm admitting to anything, but I don't understand why you're attacking me. Wasn't seeing other people your suggestion?" She shrugged her shoulders dismissively.

"Don't try to put this on me. Having recreational activities outside of our relationship is one thing. Sleeping with the boss to steal my promotion is another."

"*Your* promotion?" Sharay laughed. "I'm going to bed.

"I'm not finished.'

"Turn the lights off when you are." Sharay climbed the stairs to their bedroom.

****

Balile glanced through the two-way mirror at the young boy. He remembered when he had first learned of the children at the Center. He often wondered what would have happened if he had saved the small child under the bar. The child's face still haunted him. He would be devastated when he learned, years later, that the child had been rejected by the Center, and even more so when he would learn what happened to children the Triad rejected.

"You look surprised." The woman startled him.

"I am. I saw him shortly after he arrived. It was just before they transferred him; he was a mess."

"Now look at him. He's one of our best new recruits. It's never about how devastated they are in the beginning; it's about how quickly they adjust."

"I'm glad he made it."

"Me, too. Time is short, and we need all hands on deck, if you know what I mean. Don't get me wrong; that doesn't mean I intend to allow a bad apple to spoil my crop. This is a ruthless world, and only the strong can be allowed to survive, but I was rooting for this one. I'm just glad he was one of the strong ones."

Balile was confused. He had never seen her show any concern for the children brought to the Center. What made this one so special?

"I hear your thoughts," she said, smiling.

Balile shifted uncomfortably.

"I'm just kidding. Relax; you're safe with me. I'm just saying that I know what you're wondering. You want to know what makes Marcus special. You want to know why we would care what happens to him when we dispose of at least half of the kids we take into the Center."

That many? he thought. Balile wasn't sure he wanted to know any more.

"His parents are very prominent members of the FLOCK Some even say that his father may one day be its ranking leader. That makes Marcus a huge acquisition."

Balile felt his blood run cold. She was so beautiful, yet so deadly. No matter how reassuring she tried to be, he never got over the feeling of being in the presence of unnatural evil.

"So how is our boy doing?" she asked.

"Eric is—"

"I meant Neal. You're going to have to bring him here eventually."

"I thought he'd been to the Center before."

"He has only been to our New York office. Neither he nor his brother have been to our training facility here in Italy." She took his arm and led him to her office. "Don't worry so much. When the time comes, he'll do you proud."

****

When Prescott walked into the lab, all eyes turned toward him. The day they all had been waiting for was finally there. Prescott was going to announce his selection of the new team leader.

Eric steadied his nerves. He'd done everything right. He was sure that it would be his name that Prescott announced, but he would not relax until he heard his name.

Prescott took center position as everyone gathered close to hear the announcement. The lab had been abuzz with anticipation all day. It was just like Prescott to draw things out for dramatic effect.

"I really appreciate your all taking time from your busy schedules to allow me to address you. The selection process was a difficult one, but once made, it was obvious we'd chosen the right person was for the job. To make a long story short …"

Too late, Eric thought to himself.

"… and without further delay, I'd like to present the new head of operations here at the lab: Sharay."

The lab erupted in applause. Though many were surprised that Eric had not been selected, most preferred Sharay anyway. They all congratulated her.

"Okay, guys," Prescott interrupted. "I'm going to have to run. Sharay, I'd like for you to swing by my office this evening before you leave so that I can give you directions to my home. I plan to host an informal meeting with all the department heads concerning some of the changes I would like to implement."

"Sure."

"May I speak to you for a moment?" Eric asked Prescott before he left.

"What can I do for you?"

"Why did you lead me to believe the position was mine and then hand it to Sharay?"

"It was close, but I just felt that she was more dedicated to the lab."

"How can you say that? I've given this lab everything I had in me."

"This field is a community; there are few secrets."

"Your point being?"

"Are you going to take the New York offer?"

"I hadn't planned to." Eric tried to hide his shock. He hadn't even told Sharay about the offer. She couldn't have told Prescott, but how else could he have known?

"And now?"

"I'm keeping my options open," Eric answered defiantly.

"Exactly."

Eric was in no mood to deal with Sharay's apparent betrayal, so he stopped at a bar before heading home.

He couldn't believe how badly things had turned out. Sharay had never before aspired to run the lab. When he had first met her, she'd been a purest, loving science for knowledge's sake—but now she was his boss. He couldn't imagine in what universe this all made sense. He had noticed that she'd become increasingly ambitious. He only wished he'd realized earlier just how ambitious.

After the abortion, she'd become distant, throwing herself into her work, but he only assumed she had wanted to keep busy. All the signs had been there, but he had missed them all, and now it was too late.

As he nursed his drink, he reflected on all the mistakes he'd made that had led him to that very moment. Even if he didn't believe in God, he was beginning to believe in karma. How would their lives be different if he'd asked her to marry him instead of bullying her into having the abortion? He couldn't remember the last time he and Sharay had just enjoyed each other's company since the abortion. They had stopped calling in late just to spend a few extra moments in each other's arms, or sneaking off at lunch for a quick picnic in the backseat of the car. Now, they drove separate cars so that they weren't obligated to leave or return home together. He missed her; he missed the two of them.

Eric had an idea. He paid his tab and went to a nearby mall.

When Sharay arrived home, Eric had a candlelit dinner waiting, with a chilled bottle of champagne.

"What's all this?" Sharay asked.

"I thought we could celebrate."

"I'm surprised you're taking this so well. I had hoped you wouldn't take it personally. I'm so glad that you're happy for me. You didn't look too pleased when you left the lab."

"I was just surprised. Prescott had all but promised it to me, but how could you think I wouldn't be happy for you?"

"I was being silly. I was afraid that you'd be angry. I knew how much this promotion meant to you, but I wanted it just as badly," Sharay explained.

"So, I'm a little disappointed. I'd worked for it for so long, but I'm still very happy for you."

"Thank you."

"Don't mention it. Just enjoy the evening. That will be thanks enough." He handed her a single red rose.

Sharay was delighted. It was a little too cliché for her tastes, but she was not going to complain. It had been far too long since their last romantic evening together, and she had missed him.

Sharay knew that she had crossed the line and that he felt betrayed, but she had felt equally as betrayed by him. Maybe there was hope for them. She was ready to put the unpleasantness of the last year and a half behind them, and she was thrilled to see that he wanted the same.

After dinner, Eric led her down a rose-petal–covered hallway to their bedroom. "I got you a gift." He handed her a wrapped box.

Sharay tore into the gift like a five-year-old at Christmas. She smiled when she pulled out a negligee.

"It's your color."

She ran to the bathroom to put on the strapless, peach-colored, Oriental-print negligee. Eric reached into the nightstand drawer and pulled out a second, smaller box. When Sharay emerged from the bathroom wearing the revealing negligee, he went down on one knee with the opened box in an outstretched hand.

"What is that?" Sharay asked, sitting on the bed.

"I'd like you to do me the honor of becoming my wife."

"Oh, I see. You mean, like, settle down and make babies? Maybe take a leave of absence from the lab?"

"No, not right away."

Sharay lowered her voice to just above a whisper, but inside she was screaming. "Let me make sure I understand you. I guess you think I shouldn't go to Prescott's house tomorrow either right?" She could barely contain her anger.

"I think it sends the wrong impression."

"What impression might that be? Oh, you mean it may give the impression that I really want this job?"

"You know exactly the impression I mean. I think you should think about our relationship before you do something rash."

"I get it. You mean I should sacrifice for us?"

"You could say that."

"Never again!" she yelled. She grabbed the box and threw it across the room.

Eric scrambled to find it.

Sharay looked at Eric in disgust. His fear and ambition would always stand in the way of any real commitment. She feared that their happy ending was slipping away from them.

"I'm asking you—no, I'm telling you—if you value our relationship, you won't go. You've got the promotion. You don't have to be at Prescott's beck and call anymore."

"This is not about Prescott. This is about us. Either you trust me or you don't." She got into the bed and rolled over, turning her back to him. "I'm finished with this discussion. It's my job, and I am going. You'll have to decide what that means to our relationship."

Unable to sleep, Eric went downstairs. He could not believe that she'd do this to him. Even if she could be trusted, she had to know what everyone else would think. Every day, he felt her pulling farther and farther away from him. Soon it would be too late. Eric picked up the phone and called her sister, Angela.

He hoped he was doing the right thing. He knew how private Sharay was and that she and Angela had not been close for years, but he had to find someone who could help him fix things. He wasn't sure if that was even possible anymore, but he did know that things could not continue as they were.

"So you'll come?" Eric asked.

"Of course. My sister means as much to me as she means to you. Are you sure she won't mind? I'm not sure if she told you, but we didn't exactly end things on the best of terms."

"She didn't elaborate, but she did say that your relationship was strained. I think this is the perfect opportunity to kill two birds with one stone. Maybe your visit can fix both our relationships with your sister."

"Maybe you're right."

"I'm sure it will be fine, but just in case, I'd rather if you didn't mention any of this to her. I don't want her to shut us down without giving us a chance."

"Of course. I agree completely. Thanks again for calling me." She smiled as she hung up the phone. The Triad had ordered her to help manage the situation with Eric. Until he called, she had no idea how she was going to do that.

"Who was that?" Neal asked.

"Your brother. He wants me to talk to my sister."

"That's fortunate. Don't forget that time is a factor. The Triad wants this done quickly."

"I'm leaving first thing tomorrow. I should be there by nightfall. If he's anything like his brother, this should be a piece of cake." She brushed his lips with hers, but stopped just short of kissing him.

"Does she know you're coming?" Neal smiled.

"She will. My sister hates for me to meet her boyfriends. This should be interesting."

"Do you think that could have something to do with how you take that thing about sisters sharing too far?"

"He does have a nice voice."

"Just stay on task and remember which brother you married." He slapped her butt. He loved a sassy woman, and Angela always gave as good as she got.

****

Eric spent the entire day planning for Angela's visit. He hoped he hadn't made a mistake by inviting her. He'd taken the entire day off to cook and clean without drawing Sharay's suspicions. He planned to tell her just before picking Angela up from the airport. He figured that way she would have less time to find a way out of the visit, but when Sharay called to tell him that she would be late, he was forced to put plan B into action. He'd have to spring the visit on her after picking up Angela from the airport. It was riskier, but she'd left him with no other choice. Maybe this was better. This way she couldn't refuse the visit at all.

Angela's plane arrived early. She was impressed to find Eric waiting. She smiled as he approached. He looked so much like his brother.

"You must be Angela." He offered her his hand.

"You must be Eric." She hugged him instead. "Where's my sister? Didn't she come with you?"

"She's meeting us at the apartment."

"She still doesn't know I'm coming, does she?"

He shook his head.

"You do love to live dangerously, don't you?" Angela thought that Eric was either very brave or very stupid.

"Where is your overnight bag?" Eric asked. He'd heard of traveling light, but this was extreme.

"I'm only here for the day. My return flight leaves at midnight."

"I see."

Angela was happy to fill Eric in on all the sordid details about her and Sharay's childhood while they waited for Sharay to arrive. The more he learned, the more he realized that Sharay might be even more damaged than he was.

When Sharay got home from visiting her boss, William Prescott, she found Eric and Angela waiting for her.

"What is she doing here?" she demanded.

"We were waiting for you. Don't I at least warrant a hello?" Angela held out her arms.

"Hello, Angela. Now, what is she doing in my house?"

"I invited her. I thought maybe she could help."

"I don't need any help. If you think you need help, then feel free. Angela's always been all too happy to help my boyfriends."

"I can't believe you're still so bitter. That was a lifetime ago."

Sharay shot her a harsh glare.

Angela gave her sister a slight wink, careful not to be detected by Eric. It was important for him to believe she was there to help save their relationship, not present the final death blow.

"Why do you hate me so much?" Sharay stiffened her face, determined not let Angela see her cry.

"Why would you say that? I know things haven't always been great between us." Angela leaned over and hugged her sister. She whispered into her ear. "There you go again. This is not about you. Sticking it to you is just a bonus."

Sharay felt a cold chill run the full length of her body. She stormed out of the apartment, slamming the door behind her.

"I see she still runs away when things get heavy."

"Maybe this was a bad idea," Eric conceded.

"Maybe it was, or maybe not. Why don't you show me around the place?"

"Now?"

"Can you think of a better time? When my sister returns, I doubt she'll be in the mood."

Though baffled by her request, Eric showed Angela the apartment. As he escorted her down the hall, Angela took notice of his muscular physique. "Not bad."

"What was that?" he asked.

"My sister has always had great taste."

"Yes. She decorated this entire place herself."

"You don't say." Angela smiled as she brushed up against him. "So what has my sister told you about me?"

"Not much. I know that she blames you for destroying her last relationship, but she never mentioned any details."

"What do you think happened between us?" She gently stroked his arm.

He pulled away. "I don't know." Eric was becoming increasingly more uncomfortable by Angela's lack of respect for his physical boundaries. As he approached the bedroom, he paused.

"Anything wrong?" She smiled.

"No. This is the bedroom." Eric quickly moved to the next room. "Let me show you the den."

Angela grabbed his hand and pushed open the bedroom door.

"I think we should—" he started to protest.

She put a finger to his mouth to silence him. *This is too easy*, she thought. "Why am I really here?"

"You know why you're here. You're here to help me save my relationship."

"I doubt that. You had to have suspected why my sister and I don't get along. You can lie to me, but don't lie to yourself. That's too pathetic."

Eric opened his mouth to protest, but he knew that Angela was right. He knew that he had really dodged a bullet with Sharay's pregnancy, and he was relieved. Maybe Sharay had been right as well. He had blamed her for the distance between them and accused her of pulling away, but maybe he was just as guilty.

"You want out. I'm just your ticket." She took his hand, but he snatched it away.

"You're her sister," Eric protested.

"Tell me you don't want this to happen." She pushed him down on the bed and straddled him. "Just tell me to stop."

"I love Sharay." He pushed her off and sat up on the bed.

"Are you sure about that? You see, I think you hate her. She got your promotion by doing for Prescott what you couldn't."

"No, she didn't. She worked hard for that promotion. She deserved it as much as anyone."

"That doesn't matter, not really. The point is she took what you wanted more than anything, and you hate her for it."

"You're wrong."

"Then why are you here with me? Why didn't you run after her? The truth is you want out, and you asked me here to help you."

"That's not true. I asked you here to help save our relationship."

"Don't you get it? She's already gone. She knew that this would happen if she left us alone. It's who I am; it's what I do. We've been playing this same game since we were children. That's why she hasn't let me meet you before now."

"Maybe I am angry about the promotion, but I don't want to hurt her."

"Are you telling me that you guys are dating exclusively?"

"No."

"Whose idea was that?"

"Mine, but there are rules, and you're her sister. She'd never forgive us."

"Then don't tell her." Angela kissed his neck and stroked his upper thigh. She felt him yield to her touch. "Let me make it better. What better way to make her pay for what she's done. Remember, she betrayed you first. I guarantee you that the guilt only lasts for a moment."

Sharay walked to the park. She could not believe that of all the people Eric could have turned to for help, he had chosen to invite Angela, the person she hated most in the world. Now Angela had all the ammunition she needed against her. Now she knew everything. She knew about the baby; about her and Eric's strained relationship; and she was pretty sure Angela had figured out about her affair with her boss. She guessed Angela couldn't wait to confirm all Eric's suspicions.

She'd wanted so much to forgive him, and she thought she had, but how else could she explain what she'd done. She knew how much he wanted that promotion, but she had wanted equally as much to be the one to take it away from him. She hoped it wasn't too late. Maybe they could save what they had. She wasn't sure she was ready to marry him, but she did know she wasn't ready to give up on their relationship yet.

As Sharay made her way back to the apartment, she reminisced about the good times. How had things gotten so complicated? Eric may have screwed up royally, by going to her sister for help, but at least he was trying. If they were going to survive as a couple, they would have to learn to trust each other again.

Eric glanced at the clock as he buttoned his cuff links. He knew that what they'd done was wrong. Sharay would never forgive him if she found out about their betrayal.

"Listen up." Angela pulled on her dress and fixed the covers on the bed. "You're going to take the job in New York because it's the right thing for you both. You're going to give Sharay some time and space to figure out what she needs from you and this relationship, and you're not—I repeat, you are *not* going to confess. Trust me. This is all for the best. In a few years, you'll think back on this night and be grateful that she didn't accept your pathetic proposal. Now, let me give you a piece of advice: the next time you think you're in love, and she happens to tell you she's pregnant, do the right thing."

"Why did you do this to her?"

"You mean 'we,' don't you? I didn't tie you down and rip off your clothes." She smiled defiantly. "Well, I didn't tie you down, anyway."

He looked away. He couldn't bear the sight of her.

"It's too late for remorse now. Just get over it. You never should have been together in the first place."

"What's that suppose to mean?"

She looked at him with contempt. It was pathetic how he still feigned the poor devoted lover led astray by the evil temptress.

"I asked you a question," he said.

"Yes, you did, and I determined it was not worth dignifying with an answer." She couldn't imagine why the elders had chosen such a weak man, but it was not for her to know the minds of gods.

When Sharay returned home, she found Angela preparing to leave. A cab pulled up in front of the apartment.

"It looks like my cab is here. I'm sorry we didn't get to spend more quality time together before I had to go."

"Going so soon?" Sharay sniped.

"My plane leaves in a few hours, and I promised my husband I'd be home tonight."

Sharay felt relieved until she saw the look on Eric's face.

"I guess you got what you came for."

"I guess my work here is done." Angela smiled.

Sharay looked at Eric, but he looked away. She recognized the look on his face; it was guilt, but then she should have recognized it—she'd seen it on the faces of so many of her boyfriends before him.

"I'm glad I got to see you before I left." Angela hugged her.

Sharay pulled away. "I'm sorry I can't say the same."

"I hope to see you in New York." Angela winked at Eric.

Sharay looked at Eric.

"I'm sorry. I assumed you already knew that Eric was taking the job in New York."

"You spend less than ten hours with my sister, and she convinces you to throw away what took us so much time to build. How does that work? Can you please explain that to me?"

"I wanted to be the one to tell you about the job in New York. I received the offer weeks ago, but I wanted to wait until Prescott made his final decision.

I had hoped that tonight we could sit down and discuss matters like adults, but I think our wounds run too deep. Maybe a little distance will allow us the time we need to heal before we damage this relationship beyond repair, so don't blame Angela. She only came to help."

"I'll bet she did. I don't need space. She has no idea what I need."

"But it's what I need," Eric insisted. "And I know the time apart will be good for our relationship. I'm not leaving you. I can commute weekends." He shuffled uncomfortably. "I want to be happy about your promotion, but that can't happen with my trailing behind your accomplishments, blaming you for what I should have had the guts to go after myself. Once I feel better about where I am in my career and what I'm doing with my life, we can rebuild our relationship. I promise that things are going to work out for the best."

"You promise? Oh, well, then, I guess it's so."

"The last thing I ever wanted was to hurt you, and I don't blame you for rejecting my proposal. You had to do what you felt was best for you. I'm sorry, but I'm just doing the same thing. That may be selfish, but I have to look out for me right now."

"That may be the first real thing you've said to me tonight."

Chapter Eight

Aaron found Christopher on the rooftop, staring into space.

"So there you are," Christopher greeted him.

"Everyone's been looking for you. This is your big night. What are you doing up here alone?" Aaron asked.

Christopher held up his drink.

"I see. Nervous?"

"Are you kidding?"

Aaron laughed. "It's time to go back downstairs. The polls are closed and the early results are pouring into the stations."

"Can't we just wait until it's over?"

"No." Aaron patted Christopher on the back and nudged him toward the stairs.

"There he is!" a woman yelled as they entered the room.

"Congratulations!" A man shook his hand.

"We're proud of you, son." Christopher's mother hugged him.

"Is it over?" Christopher asked.

"Is it over?" His father laughed. "Do you believe this guy?"

"There's no way for him to catch you. It's a landslide victory. Stancil should be announcing his concession any moment," Tracy informed him.

"Thank you, Tracy."

"You're welcome, Congressman Michaels." She winked.

"I like the way that sounds." He smiled as he watched her walk away.

"I saw that," Aaron teased.

"Bad habits die hard."

"That's all well and good, but just make sure that they die," Christopher's father interrupted. "It's time to think about settling down with a good woman."

"You think maybe I can just relish the moment before I have to consider my next political move?"

"Do you mind if I borrow the congressman for a moment before he has to make his acceptance speech," Tracy interrupted. She led him to a secluded room.

"Yes, Tracy, what can I do for you?"

"Relax. I just thought you looked like you could use some rescuing."

"That's it?"

"Yes. That's it. All I want you to do for me is to enjoy tonight, because tomorrow you have more to do than you can imagine."

"Thanks, Tracy."

"No problem."

****

Eric tossed the newspaper on his desk. He wasn't surprised to see that Christopher had won by a landslide. If Christopher hadn't been so against scientific advancements, he might have voted for him. Eric sat at his desk and reached deep into the drawer. He found the ring pressed into the corner; it was still in its box. He removed it and held it up—it caught the light perfectly. He'd made the final payment just two weeks ago, and now he wondered what he should do with it. He returned it to its box and reached for the phone.

"Hello." Sharay answered.

"Are you busy?" he asked.

Sharay was surprised to hear from him so early. There was a two hour time difference, so Eric usually called her around his dinnertime, which was right around the time she left the lab. Though she was in the middle of things, she was happy to hear from him. It had been weeks since they had last spoken to each other.

"I want to talk to you about something."

"You know that you can tell me anything." Suddenly aware of the seriousness in Eric's tone, she stopped what she was doing and gave him her full attention.

"I'd like you to move here to New York. There's an opening at the lab."

"Are you kidding?"

"I just think it would be good for our relationship if we were at least on the same coast."

"We're doing fine. Why ruin things?"

"Don't you miss me?" Eric could feel the desperation in his voice. He didn't like it. "Just forget it; I was just being silly."

"I know you're lonely, and I wish I had time to discuss this with you right now, but this really isn't a good time for me. This is my busiest part of the day."

"Sorry. I'll let you go," Eric said.

"Don't be that way.'"

"No. It's fine. You're right. It was a lousy idea."

"I'll talk to you later, okay?"

"Sure." Eric hung up the phone and placed the ring into his jacket pocket. On the way home, Eric stopped into a jewelry store.

"How much will you give me for this?" Eric placed the ring onto the counter.

The jeweler eyed him suspiciously.

"I'd like to use it as a down payment for that ring." Eric pointed to a ring worth at least three times as much.

The jeweler smiled and examined the ring.

****

"Can I offer you something to drink?" the director asked Sarah.

"Yes, thank you."

"Has Eric broken things off with Sharay?"

"Not yet, but it's only a matter of time." Sarah sipped the hot coffee. She hadn't really wanted anything, but saying "yes" came as second nature. She was loyal to death.

"Eric will never fully commit to anyone else as long as she's in the picture."

"He's loyal to her, but I am sure that he's no longer in love with her. He just needs a little more time," Sarah explained.

"What can we do to help speed things along?" The director wasn't used to feeling so out of control of a situation.

"From what I've noticed, we don't have to do anything."

Sarah hated deceiving Eric. She'd been like a mother to him since his parents died, and she'd grown to care for him very much, but her love for the Triad was greater. She wasn't in the habit of saying no to the Triad, even when asked to betray someone she loved or to give up the thing that meant the most to her in the world: her daughter.

"You've done well."

"I live to serve."

"As do we all, but your personal sacrifice will not go unrewarded."

"Being able to be of service to the Triad is its own reward. I present myself and my family as living sacrifices to the master."

****

Christopher joined Tracy for dinner their first night in Washington DC. They needed to review before his first meeting with the other representatives from his party. Tracy wanted to go over what he should expect from his first party meeting, as well as his first few days in Congress. The way he began his term was crucial. It was her experience that mistakes were easier to avoid than they were to fix. Christopher simply wanted to burst on to the floor with all his big ideals, but it was her job to reinforce the need for diplomacy.

"I made a lot of promises, and I fully intend to keep them all."

"Have you ever heard of catching more flies with honey?"

"Yes, and it's a cliché." Christopher had no intention of compromising his ideals for his party or anyone else.

"It's a cliché because it's true," Tracy explained. "This meeting with the other party members is important if you plan to get anything done in this town."

"I haven't even started yet, and people already expect me to compromise."

"You don't have to agree with them, but you do have to hear them out."

"Fine," Christopher agreed.

"Now, on a lighter note ..." Tracy pulled several files from her bag. She handed them to him. "You have to select your Washington staff."

"I still don't understand why my present staff is not enough." He pushed the folders to her side of the table.

"They're in New York." She pushed the folders back to him. "I've narrowed the search to these few. I was particular impressed by the new speech writer, Kelly Airs. She came highly recommended, and her résumé is amazing."

The waiter returned with their meals.

"Whatever you think is fine. I trust your opinion completely." He picked up his fork.

"Did you want me to bless the food as well?"

Christopher sheepishly put down his fork and prayed over their dinner.

Chapter Nine

Eric tasted the sauce. He added a little sugar to lessen the tanginess of the tomatoes. He wanted everything to be perfect. He had checked her schedule, and the nurses on duty had assured him that she would be on time. He was grateful for all their help in clearing her schedule, since nothing got done around there without their blessing.

He reached into his pocket and pulled out the ring. It was understated; a nearly flawless diamond set in an elegant gold infinity band. He knew he had paid way too much for it, but he was sure that she would love it, and that was all that mattered. What it lacked in size, it more than made up for in quality. He closed the box and returned it to his pocket. There was still so much to do before she arrived.

The timer went off. Eric rotated his pie before returning to his sauce. He planned to wait until she rang the bell before dropping in the pasta; he didn't want to overcook it. Even though he was sure she'd accept his proposal, he still needed this night to be perfect. It was the night about which they would tell their grandchildren.

The phone rang.

"Hello," Eric answered. He was annoyed by the intrusion. He was running short on time, and anyone who mattered knew how important this night was for him.

"How are things going? Are you finished? Did the pie turn out right?" Sarah had tried not to call, since she knew how pressed for time he would be, but she could barely contain her excitement.

"You're worst than a mother hen," Eric teased. Though pressed for time, he was happy to hear her voice. She'd always had a calming effect on him, and he could really use that right then. "Everything is turning out just perfectly. Even the pie is cooperating. Thanks again for the recipe. You'd think a scientist wouldn't be so inept at mixing ingredients, wouldn't you? Tell me again how I'll know when it's done."

"The knife will come out clean."

"Right."

"Calm down. Don't be nervous. She loves you as much as you love her. In fact, I've never seen a woman so much in love."

"This really isn't just about the baby. I really do love her."

"I know."

"When I moved back East, I thought my life was over …" He took a deep breath. "But she showed me how incredible my life could be. I swear I never thought I could be this happy."

"You deserve to be happy. Remember that."

"I don't know about all that, but thanks. Whether I deserve happiness or not, I'm holding on to it with everything in my soul."

The doorbell rang.

"Crap! She's early." Eric hung up the phone and turned down the stove. He tidied up his appearance before opening the door. His smile faded. It was Sharay.

****

Christopher and Kelly decided to stay late to review his speech. This was his first time home in New York since going to Washington, and he was going to address his constituents for the first time since the election. It would be his most important speech thus far, and he wanted everything to go smoothly. At the last minute, Christopher had decided to bring Kelly with him. She had become his lead speech writer, and he felt most comfortable with her by his side to handle any last-minute adjustments to the speech.

"Excuse me, Congressman," his secretary interrupted. "Your mother is on line one. It sounds important."

Christopher smiled. "I forgot to call my parents when I got into town. She's probably calling to read me the riot act. Would you excuse me?" Christopher picked up the line.

Kelly slowly began to collect her things but stopped when she saw Christopher's expression darken. "Is anything wrong?" she whispered.

Christopher placed his hand over the mouthpiece and said to Kelly, "My father was just rushed to the hospital."

"I'll call for the driver."

"Thank you. I'll meet him downstairs."

"Would you like me to go with you to the hospital?"

"No. Would you call Tracy? She and my parents are extremely close."

"Sure. I'll take care of it."

Christopher rushed to meet the car. He replayed the day over and over in his head. He was supposed to have dinner with his parents when he left the office, but he'd decided to work late. He should have been there. What if this was it? What if he didn't get the chance to say good-bye?

"Would you hurry?" Christopher pleaded to the driver.

The driver darted in and out of traffic. Fortunately, traffic was light, even for that time of night. As he approached the hospital, the phone rang, and he was instructed to go to the rear of the hospital, where Tracy was waiting for them.

"Come with me. I'll take you to your dad." Tracy led him through a back entrance. "Someone must have alerted the media, because it's a madhouse out front."

"What are you doing here? I mean, how did you get here so quickly?"

"I was there when your father got sick. Your parents invited me to dinner. I think the plan was to get both of us together."

"I'm sorry about that. Subtlety was never their best suit."

"I don't mind. I'm flattered that they consider me a good match for their only son." They took the service elevator to the cardiac wing of the hospital. She led him down the hall, and they paused just outside his father's room.

"Go ahead; he's waiting for you."

Christopher slowly pushed open the door. Mitch lay on the bed with his eyes closed. He was hooked up to several monitors. Christopher hardly recognized his father. He looked so frail.

"Is he asleep?" Christopher asked.

"I was," Mitch answered.

"I'm so sorry I missed dinner."

"Let me ask you. Was it work-related?"

"Yes."

"Then you did the right thing. I'm proud of your dedication. I want you to keep pushing forward and never back down. There's no limit to what you can accomplish if you never give up."

"Don't you mean 'we'?"

"It's your turn this time."

"Don't say that."

"It's okay. I'm happy with the choices that I've made. I may not have gotten everything that I thought I wanted, but what I did get was so much better than I could have ever hoped for. You and your mother gave my life meaning. My only regret is that it took me so long to realize just how lucky I was." Mitch struggled to finish. "I should have told you something …."

"You can tell us later. Right now you need your rest. I want you to go back to sleep," Christopher insisted.

"No time but the present."

"Don't you mean that there is no time *like* the present?" Christopher asked as he adjusted his father's pillow. "I want you to rest now."

Mitch smiled. He had said exactly what he had intended to say. He knew that the present was all that they had left, and he had no intention of spending his final moments asleep. He imagined he wouldn't have much need for sleep where he was going.

Mitch smiled at Tracy, then turned his head slightly to look at Christopher. "Don't worry, son. You'll have someone far better than me by your side, and I'll never really leave you. I'll always be inside your heart." Mitch reached out for his wife.

She took his hand and lovingly gazed into his eyes.

"We did a good job," he said softly.

"We did a very good job," she agreed and gently kissed his lips. "Good night, my love."

The monitor confirmed what she already knew. He was gone. The doctors rushed into the room and began CPR, but Mitch remained unresponsive.

"I'm so sorry for your loss," the doctor said. "We tried everything, but the damage caused by the heart attack was too extensive."

"Thank you." Determined to be brave, Laura blinked away a tear. She knew that her husband would have wanted her to be strong.

"I'll give you a moment. Let us know when you're finished." The doctor excused himself.

Christopher hugged his mother. Finally, all the tears that she had been fighting broke free as she openly sobbed in his arms.

****

"Are you finding everything okay?" Eric asked with his ear pressed against the bathroom door. It startled him when she opened the door.

"You bet. Nice bathroom. Did you decorate it yourself?" Though her words were benign, her tone was not.

"Would you like a brandy?" Eric poured a drink. He offered it to Sharay. She declined. He recapped the bottle.

"Since when do you drink brandy? It's a little lightweight for your tastes, wouldn't you say?"

"I do a lot of things that I didn't used to do."

"So I see."

"When did you get in town?" he asked. "I would have met you at the airport."

"Really? I would have thought you were too busy. After all, you haven't returned any of my messages." She took his glass and downed its final drops.

"I'd wanted to do this in person."

"Well, then, I'm here; you're here. What are you waiting for?" She handed him the glass and sat across from him on the loveseat. She patted the space beside her.

"This isn't how I wanted to break this to you." Eric took the seat across from her.

Sharay leaned forward in an exaggerated display of being attentive.

"I've met someone."

Sharay leaned back confidently in her chair and crossed her legs. Her stern look softened into a slight grin.

"Don't look at me like that. Didn't you here me?" Eric was losing his patience. Of all nights for her to just show up unannounced.

"Of course I heard. You're certainly speaking loudly enough. I just don't see why there's so much drama. Since when have we deprived each other of life's little distractions?"

"This is different."

"I can see that."

"Don't be condescending."

"Nothing could be further from my intentions." She pursed her lips.

"Then don't be coy. It really doesn't suit you."

"Okay, then let's be real, since coy no longer suits me. You say this is different. Tell me how."

He tried to choose his words carefully. Though he was no longer in love with Sharay, he still did not want to cause her any unnecessary pain.

"I'm waiting," she said impatiently. "What's this really about? Are you still bitter that I got promoted over you? Really, I thought you'd gotten over this childishness."

"Of course not," Eric vehemently protested. "I admit not getting the promotion was hard, but I believe things worked out for the best. I love my new job."

"Then what?"

"This isn't about you, but knowing you the way I do, I can certainly see how you'd need to make it about you."

"Then you tell me what this is all about," Sharay demanded.

"I am. You're just not hearing me."

"Then tell me again. Help me understand all this. What is this place, this room, all this junk?" She plucked at a bowl of aroma beads.

"They're lavender aroma beads to calm my nerves."

"You know what I mean. None of this is you—not that bathroom with the matching hand towels, not that apricot brandy crap you offered me to drink, and for sure, not the lavender aroma beads. You always scoffed at this sappy form of domestication."

"It wasn't me, but I've changed."

"No one changes this much."

"You do for the right person."

"The right person? Six months ago, I was the right person. Remember, it was you who called me, begging me to give up my position at Grayson."

"That only proves that I was so afraid of the way I was feeling that I almost made one of the biggest mistakes of my life."

Sharay couldn't believe what she was hearing. "So seven years together was all a mistake?"

"No, but seven more would have been."

"You can't love her. No one falls this madly in love with someone in six months."

Eric looked away. He didn't know how to tell her. She deserved better than this.

"Oh. I get it. How long have you been seeing her?"

"Almost a year," he whispered, as if the softness of his tone would somehow lessen the blow. "We met shortly after I arrived, but I swear nothing happened until much later. It'd been so long since we'd been close, and one thing just led to another. Then I lost my apartment across town, and she helped me find this apartment in her building."

"That was so kind of her. Do remind me to thank her."

"I'm so sorry. We never expected to fall in love."

"So when you asked me to join you, you were already in a relationship with this woman? Is that what you are telling me?"

"I thought if you were here, I wouldn't feel so strongly for her. I was afraid of how close Katelyn and I had become," he explained.

"Katelyn? What the heck kind of bimbo name is Katelyn?"

"Her name is Dr. Katelyn Knight. She's a pediatric surgeon at the local hospital. Sarah introduced us. We never planned this; it just happened. I can't explain it, but … we're getting married."

"Married? When?"

"In a month."

"When were you going to tell me? Were you going to send me an invitation or just mail me a postcard from your honeymoon?"

"I wanted to wait until after your birthday."

"How thoughtful. I guess I should be grateful that you didn't just send me an e-mail."

"I wouldn't do that to you. I didn't mean for you to find out like this. You deserve so much better than that."

"Thanks. That means so very much to me right now. Let me ask you: why the huge rush?" Sharay pressed.

"We're … expecting."

"Expecting what? A child? This night just keeps getting better."

"This is why I wanted to wait to tell you. I knew how upsetting this would be, especially after the whole baby thing."

"Don't. You don't have a right to mention my child to me, and don't pretend that you have any idea about how I feel. You're both doctors. How could you have let this happen?"

"We weren't trying to *not* get pregnant."

"Come again?" She could not believe her ears. Was he telling her that he wanted this child? That he had planned this child? Hadn't he been the one adamant about not wanting to be a parent, ever? "You don't want children. You told me that yourself."

"Katelyn wants a family, and I want to make her happy."

"You're not hearing me. You don't want children. You sure as heck didn't want ours."

"This time it's different. I'm different."

"Why?" she pleaded. She knew she should let it go, but she had to know. "Why is this so different?"

"I love her."

"Wow." She clutched a clenched fist to her chest. She felt as if he had struck her hard enough to stop her heart.

"I didn't mean that the way it sounded."

She held up a trembling hand to stop him.

"Of course I loved you."

"Just not enough, right?"

Eric wanted to say the right thing, but nothing seemed right. He had wanted to not hurt her anymore than he already had, but everything he did seemed to cause her more pain.

"I am so sorry I came. I knew something, or someone, had come between us, but I was sure that if I came, you would remember why you fell in love with me. That was pretty naïve, huh?"

He leaned forward to comfort her, but she pulled away. She grabbed her coat and hurried to the door.

"At least allow me to call you a cab."

"No. You've done quite enough." Suddenly, she felt ill and bolted toward the bathroom.

Eric listened at the door. He could hear her crying. Part of him wanted to comfort her, while the rest of him was hoping she would hurry and leave before Katelyn got home.

As Eric watched her pull away in the taxi, he wrote the final chapter to his past.

****

Though grateful for the time he spent with Tracy and his mother in New York right after his father's death, Christopher was happy to be back in Washington DC. His secretary briefed him on his day's schedule.

"Senator McIntyre would like you to join him for lunch. Should I confirm?" she asked.

McIntyre was a New York senator serving his fifth term in the Senate. Before that, he had served in the House for two terms, and he had been on a short list for vice president last term. In the political arena, he was a superstar.

"Yes, of course. Arrange my schedule around it."

"Yes."

"That'll be all for now. Would you please close the door behind you?"

"Yes."

Christopher sat down at his desk and began to review what was on the House's agenda for the day, but his mind kept returning to Senator McIntyre's invitation. He'd attended Mitch's funeral, which was expected, but a lunch invitation from a senior senator was completed unexpected.

From his agenda, Christopher saw that the House was voting on a bill increasing the scrutiny of labs doing stem-cell research. The new law clarified when and from where these cells could be obtained, and it had stiff enough penalties for violators to give it bite. Christopher wondered if that was what McIntyre wanted to discuss. He knew that the bill had originated from the senator's office. Christopher pulled himself together. He'd have to hurry if he didn't want to miss the lunch.

McIntyre was already there when he arrived.

Christopher was unusually quiet. He wanted to allow McIntyre to begin the conversation.

"How was your first day back at work?" McIntyre asked.

"It's all been a bit overwhelming, but in a good way."

"I know the feeling."

Christopher couldn't wait any longer. He had to know why he'd been invited to lunch. "I was surprised by your invitation."

"I've been watching you for some time," McIntyre explained. "I thought it was time for us to finally get to know each other."

"I haven't been in the House that long."

"I've been watching your career since you ran for councilman a few years ago. I was impressed by your platform. I told my wife then that if you accomplished half of what you promised, it wouldn't be long before you joined me in Washington."

"It means a lot to me that you're impressed by something I said."

"It's more than what you said; it's what you did. You devoted yourself to keeping as many of your promises as you could. Anyone can make a promise." McIntyre drank the rest of his water and set the glass on the edge of the table.

Christopher noticed how close the glass was to the edge, but he didn't attempt to move it.

"Promises are like this empty glass." McIntyre pointed to the glass. He gently brushed against it, and it crashed to the floor and shattered.

A waiter rushed to their table to clean up the large pieces, crushing the smaller shards under his feet as he rushed to retrieve a small hand vacuum.

McIntyre continued. "Promises made without the weight of conviction are like an empty glass. Easily broken and even more easily forgotten. Do you agree?"

"I do."

"This is something we both share, and you will find that here in Washington, we are in the minority."

Chapter Ten

Christopher held the umbrella over Tracy as she exited the car. He didn't mind getting wet when it was for such a worthy cause. The valet rushed over to help. Christopher reached into his pocket and grabbed his wallet before relinquishing his keys. "Please take care of my baby," he whispered to the valet as he handed him the keys and an obscenely large tip.

"No problem, Senator." The man smiled. He knew if he did a good job there'd be even more money when he returned the car in mint condition.

Christopher and Tracy hurried into the restaurant. The night was dreary, but nothing could spoil their special night. It was exactly one year ago when they had said their "I do's," and tonight they were returning to the restaurant where he'd proposed to her. It had been raining on that night as well.

"Good evening, Senator and Mrs. Michaels. Right this way." The hostess immediately escorted them to the best table in the restaurant. Christopher enjoyed great service, and he didn't mind paying for it. He'd made all the arrangements himself, weeks ago. He wanted their first anniversary to be just as special as the night he'd proposed to her at that very table. The waiter immediately brought out a bottle of champagne.

Tracy looked at him lovingly when she realized how much trouble he'd gone through to duplicate the night he proposed, right up to the smallest detail. He was a wonderful husband, and she felt lucky to have him. She felt so safe with him. She knew she could trust him with her heart.

Christopher spared no expense. She was worth it. It was hard being the wife of a political figure. It took a special woman to handle always being in the public eye and having her every decision—past as well as present—held up to scrutiny, but she handled it with such poise and grace. She was amazing, and he felt lucky to have her in his life.

All the way home from dinner, Tracy basked in the glow of the evening. It had been a perfect night.

"I have wonderful news," Christopher said.

"I'm sorry, sweetheart. What did you say?"

Christopher smiled. "You look like you were a million miles away."

"I'm sorry. I was just thinking about how lovely everything was."

"We can talk about this later." Christopher decided that this might be the wrong time to have a serious discussion with her. The evening had gone so perfectly, and the last thing he wanted to do was to disrupt her good mood and possibly derail what was promising to shape up into an even better night.

"Too late," Tracy said. "Now you've piqued my interest."

"I got a call from McIntyre. Now that he's lost his running mate, God rest his soul, he's asked me to join his ticket."

Tracy was silent.

"This isn't how I wanted to tell you, but it's been driving me nuts all night. I just had to tell you. We don't have to make a decision right away."

Tracy leaned over and kissed him.

"What was that for?"

"Only you would put the future president of our country on hold to make sure your wife was okay with your running for vice president. Of course I'm fine with this. This is what you've been working your whole life to accomplish. I'm so proud of you."

Christopher pulled into their driveway. He could not wait until they got out of the car. He drew her into his arms.

****

Eric pulled into the recreation center and began unloading the equipment. As the new head coach of his son's little league team, making sure the equipment arrived on time was just one of his new duties. Until he found an assistant, he was responsible for everything, but he didn't mind one bit. After working as an assistant coach for the previous two years, he had been thrilled when he was voted head coach.

"Are you excited?" Katelyn smiled and fixed his collar. He never ceased to amaze her. He was one of the premier researchers in his field, and yet still he managed to make time to coach their son's little league team.

"What do I have to be excited about?" Eric pretended to wipe sweat from his forehead with a trembling hand.

"I know you're ready. I'm just saying …."

"I know, and yes, I'm a little nervous. I want the boys to play well. I feel like they're looking to me for inspiration, and I just don't want to let them down."

"You won't. You're a wonderful coach and an amazing leader. Win or lose, they're fortunate to have you."

"You think we're going to lose?" Eric started to protest.

Katelyn clamped her hand over his mouth. "Stop worrying! You're a great coach. I don't care what they say."

One of the players called out to him. "Coach! Do you want us to help you with the equipment?"

"Sure, that'd be great. Get Talen to help you." Eric looked around to see where his son, Talen, had gone. "Has anyone seen him?"

"He's lying in the backseat."

Eric found Talen lying in the backseat of the car and decided to let him rest until time for the game. He'd been up late with a headache but had seemed fine that morning. After unloading all the equipment, Eric sent one of the players to retrieve Talen.

"Where's my son?" Katelyn inquired before heading to her seat.

"He was tired, so I let him rest a few extra minutes."

"Coach! I can't wake up Talen!" the young boy yelled as he ran back to the field.

Katelyn's expression changed to concern as they ran to check on their son.

Eric pulled him out of the car and laid him on the ground.

"Talen! Talen, wake up. It's Mommy. I need you to try to open your eyes," Katelyn pleaded.

"What can I do?" another parent asked.

"Call an ambulance. Tell them that his breathing is shallow and that he is unresponsive." She knelt beside her son and cradled his head. She watched the slight rise and falling of his little chest.

****

The man stood in the doorway to the dormitory. He watched the young men prepare for the day's activities and wondered which one he was there to find. These were the corps' top specimens. They received the best food and lodging, but despite all their perks, he didn't envy them.

"Marcus Allen!" he called.

The young men jumped to attention as they had been trained to do.

"Marcus Allen, step forward. You have been summoned by the board."

Marcus felt his legs weaken. He struggled to maintain his composure. Showing weakness would assure his being deemed obsolete and lead to his ultimate termination. Each breath was labored.

"Follow me."

Marcus followed the man to the adjacent building where he knew the board held its meetings.

"Are you sure you have the right guy? Do you have any idea what they want with me?" Marcus asked.

The man continued down the corridor until they arrived at the door to the boardroom. He knocked.

"Come in."

Marcus tried to still his nerves, but it felt as if ants were crawling all over his body. He began to scratch.

"Be still," the man ordered.

"They'll see you now." The receptionist motioned toward the door.

Marcus struggled with each step. His legs felt like lead.

"Hello, Marcus. Have a seat."

"Thank you." Marcus shifted uncomfortably in the chair. The bright light above his head forced him to squint to make out the faces of the three-member panel—two women and an older gentleman. He could not imagine why he had been summoned, but he was sure it wasn't for anything good. It was unusual to be asked to appear before the board, and as far as he knew, it was never a good thing. Typically, this was reserved for those who betrayed the Triad.

The older gentleman handed a folder to one of the women. After reviewing its contents, she offered it to the other woman, who declined.

Marcus knew better than to speak before being spoken to, but the wait was unbearable. He wished they would just get on with things. If he'd committed some offense, then he just wished they would confront him.

"Relax. You've been summoned because the Triad has need of a favor. If you are successful, you will be handsomely rewarded. Failure, however, is not an option," the man explained.

"I understand."

"We knew you would. You are one of our top cadets. This is your file." The man indicated the file they had been reviewing. "It has every aspect of your career with us recorded on its pages. Do you know what else it has?"

"No."

"It tells us about your life before you came to the Center. It tells me about who you were and who your parents are."

Marcus could not hide his shock. He'd always been led to believe that his parents had been killed when he was taken from the park. He couldn't believe that they were still alive. Were they looking for him? Did they believe he was dead?

"Do you need a moment?" one of the women asked.

"No. I'm fine."

"Good, then let's talk about your mission."

****

Sharay didn't like surprises, least of all ones she didn't plan. When her husband, Colten Prescott, had invited one of the lab's largest supporters to dinner without warning her, she was not at all pleased.

"He doesn't care what we're having for dinner; he just wants to meet you."

"Why?"

"Why does it matter? He supports our research, both financially and in Congress, where it really counts. That should be enough of a reason for you. If it's not, fake it."

"I didn't say I wouldn't meet with him. I'm just confused. Wouldn't it make more sense to meet with the entire team at the lab? He could get a firsthand look at our progress. I just don't understand why he wants to meet with just me. Why does he feel like meeting me is so important?"

"You underestimate yourself," a voice from behind them protested. They turned to see their dinner guest.

"Sharay, let me introduce you to Senator Balile."

"It's my pleasure, Senator." She extended her hand.

"The pleasure is all mines. I've kept up with the work you've been doing, and we are extremely interested in the progress your lab has made. To answer your question, we know that you are the driving force behind its success."

After dinner, Balile and Sharay took a walk to the lake.

"Do you believe in God, Mrs. Prescott?"

"Is that a prerequisite?"

"Not at all." He found her bluntness endearing. "Your research holds much promise for the world."

"Yes, but we've reached an impasse. We're being blocked at every turn by congressional and international laws."

"You can't let that stop you."

"What can we do? We've already pushed the envelope to its limits."

"Rip it open!"

Sharay instinctively looked around. "What do you mean?"

"Don't worry. This is not a setup. We would like to help you."

"Financially?"

"Yes, but so much more. We are working to change things. We want to make your job easier by removing some of those obstacles."

"Congress is just one of our hurdles," Sharay told him. "It's obvious that Senator McIntyre is going to be our next president, and he's one of the opposition's greatest supporters. He has drawn an immovable line in the sand, and there is no way he's backing down."

"He's just one man. If he insists on standing in the way of progress, we move him."

"What about public sentiment and international prohibitions?"

"We work to change people's minds by showing them how your research can affect their lives for the better."

"That takes time," Sharay argued.

"Until then, we do what we have to do. The last time I checked, our country was still sovereign."

"Are you serious?"

"I think a better question is, are you? What are you willing to do to make this work?"

"As you said, whatever it takes."

She was one of the most driven people he'd ever met. He was impressed. They continued to walk as she explained how her research was going to change the world by not just extending life but also by improving the quality of that life.

****

Aaron and Jennifer watched their son, Justin, sleep. They could not believe he was five. It seemed like only yesterday they were rushing to the hospital for his birth.

"Happy birthday, baby," Jennifer whispered.

"We did well, huh?" Aaron hugged her and quietly pulled the door closed.

"I think we did."

"It was really nice of Tracy and Christopher to come."

"Of course they'd come. You're Christopher's best friend, and they're Justin's godparents." Jennifer headed toward their bedroom.

"I know, but now that he's running for vice president as McIntyre's running mate, everyone's been demanding his time. I'm just saying, that I would have understood if he couldn't have made it."

"Yes, but you would have been disappointed. Besides, Christopher wouldn't forget the people who are most important to him." She began dressing for bed.

"Going to bed?" Aaron sat on the bed and pulled her to him. "I thought we could sit outside and watch the stars."

"I have an early morning. Tomorrow is the Sisters-n-Christ tea and I'm expected to be there. Being the wife of an assistant pastor comes with great responsibility."

Aaron smiled. He kissed the palm of her hand.

"All right, I'll go, but just for a little while. I don't want to look tired. I need to be at my best."

"Whether you are tired or well rested, you always look amazing." Aaron led her to the patio where he had prepared a candlelit table.

Jennifer was shocked. When had he found the time to do all this?

"I know how crazy things have been lately. Between my increased responsibilities at the church and all the hours I've been devoting to FLOCK business. I'm afraid I've been neglecting you."

"I know how important your work is to you."

"Not more important than you and Justin." He put on their favorite song and took her hand in his. "Dance with me."

Aaron pulled her to him. She melted into his arms and lay her head on his shoulder as they gently rocked to the music.

****

"Mommy," Talen mumbled.

The small voice startled Katelyn. She and Eric had been keeping vigil at their son's bedside for two days.

"How are you, sweetie?" she asked her son as she leaned across him to call for a nurse.

Talen tried to sit up but was restrained by the cords from the monitors.

"Relax, honey. Let me help you." She pushed the cords to the side. "How do you feel?"

"My arm hurts." Talen held out his right arm. Suddenly he winced in pain and dropped it to his side.

"Eric," Katelyn nudged him.

"What!" He awoke, startled. "Is he okay?"

"He's awake."

"Hey you." Eric leaned over his son.

A nurse hurried into the room. Katelyn held a single finger up to her mouth to silence the woman before motioning her into the hall.

"I want you to let Dr. Phillips know that my son is awake."

"Yes, Doctor." The woman hurried to find Dr. Phillips.

So far, all Talen's tests had revealed no clue to the cause of his sudden illness. Now that Talen was awake, Katelyn hoped that he would be able to relate some unknown injury or hidden symptoms that could lead to some answers.

When Dr. Phillips arrived, he examined Talen. His symptoms suggested some form of interference in his nervous system, but all the usual suspects had been disproved. Each test had led to further tests, each less beneficial than the one before it. The source and remedy to Talen's illness remained a mystery. Dr. Phillips' exam did little to change this.

"What do you think?" Katelyn asked.

"With the exception of the small mass I showed you on his x-ray, we can't find anything unusual," Dr. Phillips explained to the frightened parents.

"What's next? Where do we go from here?" Eric wasn't used to feeling so helpless. He needed to do something. He needed to feel useful.

"I'd like to remove the mass. I know this sounds extreme, but at least once we have gotten this thing out of him, we can run the proper tests on it. We'll be able to determine if this is the source of our problems, or rule it out once and for all. I don't want you to worry; this type of surgery is fairly common."

"When would you do it?" she asked. Though she trusted him completely, she knew that brain surgery could never be considered routine.

"I would like to do it as soon as possible—today, if that's all right. I can assemble a team within the hour."

"Why so fast?" Eric asked.

"He's stable right now, but there's no way to predict what effect waiting would have. What ever caused his systems to begin to shut down was fast-moving. If we don't do something to at least slow the progress of this illness, we could lose him next time."

Katelyn struggled with the doctor side of herself that fully appreciated the seriousness of the situation, and the mother side of herself that needed to believe that everything was going to be okay. "I understand. Can you give us a few moments alone with our son?"

"Yes, of course I can. I'll get the team together."

"Thank you." Katelyn shook his hand. She knew that Phillips was at the top of his field and that they were fortunate to have him, but she could not suppress her increasing feelings of anxiety.

Eric and Katelyn went to prepare their child, while Dr. Phillips made a call.

"Hello."

"Hello. This is Dr. Eugene Phillips."

"Yes, Eugene, how's the boy."

"Not good. I'm going to have to remove the disk."

"Are you crazy? Do you know what it took to implant that disk in the first place? Besides, we have no idea what removing it at this point will do."

"I know what will happen if I don't."

"You always knew this was a possibility. We've come too far to just start over. The Triad will never consent to that. We have to let things play out."

"I can't accept that." Phillips knew the risk, but he also knew the penalty if he allowed Talen to die. "There may be another choice. I can remove the device, and monitor him and handle his meds myself."

"Don't let us down. My nephew is very important to the movement. We can't afford any mistakes at this juncture. Too many things are already in place," Neal warned.

"You can count on me." He hung up the phone and went to assemble his team.

Katelyn listened as Dr. Phillips discussed Talen's surgery with his surgery team.

"I need to be kept in the loop," Katelyn insisted.

"Of course, but you'll have to give us space," Dr. Phillips insisted. "Let us do our job."

"He's my son!"

"I know. That's why you can't be too involved. You're too close; you can't be objective."

She wanted to protest, but she knew he was right. She trusted them to do what was best, and right now, keeping her out of the operating room was best.

"As soon as we know more I'll send someone out."

"Thanks." Katelyn watched as the doors to the operating room closed before returning to the waiting room.

"What happened?" Eric looked bewildered. "I thought you were going to scrub in."

"You were right. They said I was too involved. They kicked me out." She collapsed into tears. He held her in his arms.

****

Marcus walked into the police station. This was his first time in a police station, so he was not sure what was considered the proper procedure to report a crime. He watched as both officers and civilians buzzed around him. He waited patiently for his turn, until an officer noticed him standing by the door and directed him to an intake officer.

"Can I help you?" the intake officer asked, without looking up from the documents he was sorting.

"I would like to report a kidnapping." Marcus' voice was just above a whisper.

"Whose?" The officer looked up from his papers.

"Mine."

****

Neal could feel the pounding of his heart as he and Balile made their way to the downtown office building that housed the offices of the Triad. This was his first time visiting the Triad's home base in Rome. He wanted to speak, but his tongue felt two sizes too large and clung to the roof of his mouth. He took a sip of the lukewarm water he'd been nursing for the last hour.

Balile pulled into the parking garage. Even after thirty-some years, he still felt the hairs on his arms stand up. It was as if the air surrounding the building was charged with the kind of static electricity present just before a huge thunderstorm. He wondered if Neal could feel it. He could only imagine what was going through Neal's mind. He didn't envy him one bit.

As they approached the building, the security cameras tracked their progress. Neal felt hundreds of eyes upon them. Balile reached for the door, and a woman buzzed them into the office.

"Good morning, Senator."

"Good morning, Jessica."

"The director is waiting for you in conference room B."

Balile lead Neal down the corridor to the conference room. He paused before opening the door to give Neal a moment to catch his breath. Meeting with a member of the Triad was always a life-changing event.

"Welcome home, Jeremy." The woman greeted Balile with a kiss on both cheeks. Her smile was warm and inviting.

Neal felt himself relax. He wasn't sure why Balile had made such a fuss. He couldn't imagine that such a beautiful woman could evoke fear and concern in anyone, least of all someone as formidable as the senator. Maybe he had been expecting someone else.

"Hello, Neal." As if hearing his thoughts, she turned her attention to him. "Have a seat."

"Thank you." Neal took the seat across from her.

She leaned forward to brush a strand of hair from his face, thereby revealing more of her ample cleavage. Neal felt himself stir. He wanted her. He tried to hide his excitement, but when she moved in closer, he realized it was already too late. He shifted uncomfortably. Her knee brushed his.

"You should never prejudge a person. It puts you at a disadvantage," she whispered into his ear, just before softly kissing him on the lips.

Neal felt a shiver run the length of his spine.

"Are you okay?" She stroked his hand.

"Yes. You just startled me." Neal wanted to move his hand away but it had gone limp. He tried to stand, but his legs lacked the strength to hold him. The air around him became as heavy as if a wet blanket had been placed around his shoulders. He felt huge beads of sweat racing down the sides of his face. He struggled to breathe, but each breath was more labored than the last.

"Throughout history, there has been nothing more deadly than the kiss, wouldn't you agree? Kings have fallen, saviors have been betrayed, and wars have been waged, all at the whim of such a small, seemingly benign thing as the kiss. You would do well to remember that." Her eyes turned cold, and her smile went rigid. She appeared to have been transformed into something quite terrible. Everything within him screamed for him to run, but he could not will his legs to move.

"Don't worry. I don't want you dead. I just wanted your full and undivided attention. Do you think I have that now?" She returned to the chair behind her desk.

He nodded.

"Good." She smiled. "Let's get started."

****

Scott Allen stood in the kitchen, cradling the telephone receiver. He could not bring himself to hang up the phone. He watched his wife, Mary, preparing lunch as he considered just what he was going to tell her.

"Are you all right?" Mary asked. "You look as if you've seen a ghost."

Scott opened his mouth to explain, but he could not find the words. He took her by the hand and led her to the kitchen table.

"Will you sit with me for a moment?"

"Just say it." She braced herself for whatever news he could not bring himself to tell her.

"That was Officer Kagan on the phone. Do you remember him?"

"How could I not? He inherited Marcus' case." She felt herself begin to shake. She willed herself not to cry as tears stung the corners of her eyes. She had long ago accepted that Marcus would never return home, and she had managed to gain some solace in the fact that they would one day be reunited in glory. Why would the officer call after so many years? She could not imagine what news he could have for them. Had they found her son's body?

Scott blinked back tears of his own. He took her hands in his.

"It's okay. You can tell me." She forced a reassuring smile.

"They found him."

"I thought so, but who can truly be prepared for this day. At least we can finally lay our son to rest." The tears she'd been stifling finally broke free and streamed freely down her cheeks.

"No, you've misunderstood. They found him alive—or should I say, he found them. He just walked into the police station, right off the street."

"Are they sure?" She was afraid. She had not dared to hope for so much.

"They want to run the DNA before they're sure, but they feel pretty certain that it is him."

"Thank you, Lord Jesus." She fell into her husband's arms, and they wept.

****

Callahan watched through the double-glass mirror at the young man giving his statement to the officer.

"What am I watching?" he asked the detective.

"He says he was kidnapped."

"So why did you call me? I haven't handled any kidnapping cases in years."

"He says his name is Marcus Allen. I looked it up, and you were the lead detective on the case." He handed Callahan the old file on Marcus' disappearance. "What can you tell me?"

"I remember the case well. Are you sure it's him?"

"We've already contacted his parents for DNA testing, but his story seems creditable."

"How can I help?"

"I heard this was the case that kept you awake at night."

"Eight boys go missing without a trace within a fourteen-month period. There were ritualistically mutilated animals found near each of the crime scenes with the words 'THE RECKONING' carved into each corpse. We later found the badly beaten and strangled bodies of three of the boys, and then nothing. It's the stuff of nightmares."

"There are a lot of holes in his story. We hoped you could help fill in the blanks until we get more definitive answers."

"Of course I'd like to help. What has he told you so far?"

"Very little."

"Are the other boys alive?"

"We haven't gotten that far yet."

Chapter Eleven

Aaron held out his glass to toast Christopher and McIntyre's victory. It had been a hard-fought win, and Aaron felt privileged that Christopher had chosen to share such a special moment with him and his family.

"Thanks, guys." Christopher slapped Aaron on the back.

"For what? I was just thinking how great it was of you to invite Jen and me here to celebrate with you and Tracy."

"You've got to be kidding me. Who else would we want with us? We would not have had it any other way. You guys are like family to us. We appreciate you guys sticking by us though some extremely difficult times." Christopher knew how hard things had been on all of his friends. When some of the opposing candidates had targeted his less-than-spotless past, they had gone after several of his old friends, as well as some of his new ones. Most couldn't withstand the scrutiny and chose to distance themselves. He really appreciated Aaron and Jennifer standing by them, especially after his father died.

"Excuse me, I'll be heading home." Christopher's new lead speech writer Kelly Airs interrupted. "Congratulations, again, sir."

"Thank you, Ms. Airs."

Kelly lingered a moment before closing the door behind her.

"What was that?" Aaron wasn't sure, but he thought he detected a moment between Christopher and his speech writer.

"What are you talking about? She's just a sweet kid." Christopher brushed off the implication of impropriety.

"She may be a lot of things, but 'a kid' is not one of them. Be careful. You have a lot to lose."

"Not that I would ever be so stupid as to get caught cheating on my wife, but I doubt anyone would care."

"Don't fool yourself, but I wasn't talking about the American people; I was talking about your wife and child," Aaron said.

"Oh." Christopher felt embarrassed that he'd thought of his career before his family. "I knew what you were saying."

"Yeah, right."

"I'd never cheat on Tracy. She's the only woman I've ever loved."

"Just don't lose sight of what's important. What good is saving the world if you lose the people who make it worth saving?"

"Words to live by."

Tracy and Jennifer joined the two men in the den after putting the children to bed. Tracy leaned over Christopher and kissed his cheek.

"Are the children asleep?" Christopher asked, pulling her onto his lap.

"Yes, sir, Mr. Vice President, sir. So is your mother." She giggled. "Can I do anything else for you?"

"Not now; we have company."

"Christopher!" Tracy blushed and punched his arm.

"You asked."

"You are so bad," Jennifer added in support of her friend. "What are you going to do with him?"

"I just don't know where he gets it. It's so hard to raise good husbands in the twenty-first century."

"Tell me about it."

"Hey," Aaron protested. "Leave me out of this."

"Have you asked him?" Tracy asked Christopher.

"Not yet. I was working up to it."

"'Working up to what?'" Aaron was suddenly curious. He couldn't imagine what Christopher could possibly have to ask him that required him to "work up to it."

"McIntyre asked me to give some thought to whom I would like to speak at the inauguration ceremony, and you came to mind. Now, I don't want you to feel obligated."

"Are you serious?" Aaron could not hide his enthusiasm.

"I'm very serious. You have been a staunch supporter of our campaign and our policies from the beginning, and you were an incredible asset to us when it came time to rally the Christian vote. I couldn't think of a more appropriate speaker. I'd love you to handle the prayer. It was those prayers that kept me going when things looked pretty bleak."

"Amen to that," Tracy agreed.

"I don't know what to say."

"Sure, you do. Say you'll do it," Tracy encouraged him.

"That should go without saying; but just in case it doesn't, I'd really love to speak at the inauguration ceremony."

****

"Everything is going as planned," the man reassured Balile.

Balile could not help but be concerned. Had the Triad decided to betray him? Why else would he have been instructed to campaign against McIntyre, despite the party's obvious support of him? Why had the Triad allowed McIntyre to be elected when their agendas were in direct opposition?

"I don't see how allowing McIntyre to run the country serves our purpose. He has never tried to hide his moralistic pro-Christian agenda."

"Allowing McIntyre to win the election is not the same thing as allowing him to run the country."

"You think you can control him? How? He doesn't need our support, and you'll never be able to get enough dirt on him to sway him. The man's a choirboy. He does what he believes is right, and he's always voted his conscious. His own party doesn't dictate his vote. I just don't see how allowing McIntyre to take office serves our purpose."

"Has the Triad ever failed to do exactly what it has promised?"

"Of course not." Balile lowered his voice. He hadn't intended to challenge the Triad.

"Do you think that we have lost control of this situation?"

"I'm sure you haven't."

"Then why are we having this conversation? Why are you worried?" The man was obviously annoyed.

"I just don't understand. Why have me openly declare war on the guy and then allow him to win the election? Trying to intervene now is like trying to unring a bell. Essentially, his being in office weakens my position in Congress. It makes me vulnerable to anyone trying to get into his good graces, and unlike your boy McIntyre, my closet isn't so squeaky clean."

"Don't worry. McIntyre's days are numbered. Faith is belief in the face of evidence to the contrary. It is important for it to appear that we do not oppose him. When the time is right, we will deal with him. Wait, and you'll see. Everything will work out in the end, but you must keep the course," he reassured Balile.

Balile nodded. He hoped that everything would work out, but he held no illusions. He'd worked with the Triad long enough to know that you only had their support and protection as long as it served their agenda. He was beginning to believe that his usefulness may have run its course.

"What else is bothering you? What aren't you asking me?"

Balile was reluctant to expound. The last thing he wanted was to be labeled a problem, especially when his own status was so precarious.

"It's okay; you can speak your mind." Reading Balile's concerns, he tried to appear empathetic. "Nothing you say here will be used against you."

"What about the little boy?"

"Talen?"

"How long can this continue before his little body just gives up? Or is that the plan?"

"I honestly don't know. I don't pretend to understand any of this. What I do know is that there will be casualties in this war, and sides will have to be chosen."

"Hasn't everything we've done thus far been to bring this child into the world? Isn't that why we've done all this? Isn't this child important?" Balile continued to press for answers.

"Mary from the Bible was important until she gave birth; then she was just another woman."

"What does that mean?"

"I don't have an answer. All I can do is to follow orders, just like you. We have to trust in the master's divine plan."

The problem with that was that Balile wasn't a believer. He was an opportunist, and he wasn't okay with sacrificing everything that he'd worked so hard to gain for the 'master' or anyone else.

****

Eric left the symposium completely frustrated. He had hoped to find someone doing research that might prove beneficial to finding a cure for his son. Understanding that researchers were hard pressed to devote limited resources to researching such a rare illness was not the same as accepting it. Eric would not accept that nothing could be done, simply because not enough children had died.

"Eric?"

Eric turned to see who had called his name. It was Sharay. He hadn't seen her in years, and she looked amazing.

"I can't believe it's you. I gave up running into you at one of these things a long time ago. We all thought you must have fallen off the face of the earth." She kissed one cheek and then the other.

"Hi. It's great to see you, Sharay. You look wonderful. How are things?"

"They are what they are. So how have you been? How's the family?" She tried to smile, but only managed a slight grin.

"Great."

"Well, that's wonderful."

"It's also a lie. Things aren't great. My son is dying from a rare illness, and I've proven little use in helping him. I've spent my whole life researching ways of helping people live longer, healthier lives, but when it comes time to save my own child, I prove inept. How ironic is that?"

"I'm so sorry. I didn't know."

"No, I'm sorry. How could you have known? I should not have just dumped all that on you."

"I asked how you were."

"Yes, but you don't have time to hear me vent."

"I'll make time. Is there anything I can do to help?" She touched his hand, comfortingly.

"Maybe there is something. Do you have a few minutes?"

"I was heading back to the hotel. They have a wonderful restaurant on the top floor. We could have lunch together and talk about what I can do to help."

Eric wasn't completely comfortable with the suggestion to have lunch at her hotel, but because he had not found a single lab willing to help, including his own, he was desperate. "That sounds like a plan."

As they walked to the hotel, Eric told Sharay about Talen's sudden illness and how he'd been forced to relinquish his position as the lab's top researcher to search for a cure.

He was surprised when he and Sharay arrived at his own hotel for lunch. Because his decision to attend the symposium had come at the last moment, he'd been unable to find a hotel near the convention center. The main hotels that were used by the convention had been booked for months by people in town for the festivities. He began to suspect that their encounter had been less than coincidental, but he kept his suspicions to himself. The hostess led them to a table near the window.

"So where are you staying?" She asked.

"Here in the hotel," he answered, though he was convinced that she already knew.

"How's your research going?"

"Not too well. I've devoted everything to finding a cure for my son, and my resources are depleted. I've called in every favor I had. Now that the grants have all been pulled, I'm in serious danger of losing my job. The lab isn't going to keep devoting limited resources without the promise of a big payoff."

"Science can be so callous."

"I can't blame them. They've already devoted more time and money to this than I had any right to ask. I'd have shut me down long ago, if I'd been in their position."

"They're smart. They don't want to lose you."

"I don't know about that, but my research had just begun to yield promising results, which makes shutting me down now all the more difficult to understand. If this had happened six months—even six weeks ago—it would have made more sense."

"Did they at least give you an explanation?" She tried to be sympathetic, which, to her surprise, was not difficult to do.

"Only that the lab has chosen to move in a new direction. They say that a new, more lucrative project has only recently become available and that it will require the lab's full resources. This might sound paranoid, but it's as if someone is working against me."

"I'm so sorry. I want you to know that you will always have a place at Grayson." She touched his hand lightly. It made him uncomfortable, but he fought the instinct to pull away.

He knew how badly he'd hurt her on their last encounter and that this might just be her way of getting even. Still, he had no choice but to allow things to unfold at her pace. If there was any chance that she could help him, he didn't dare risk turning her down. If there was going to be a price to pay for her help, he was fully prepared to pay it. He accepted it—from that moment on, she'd be in charge of what happened or didn't happen between them.

"From what you've told me about the direction you were going with your research, I think what I'm working on now could really benefit you. You really should take a look for yourself. You could visit the lab right after the holiday."

"Are you sure Prescott won't mind? I heard you guys got married a few years ago."

"He's my husband, not my keeper. Besides, you and I are just good friends. He knows that he has nothing to worry about."

"If you're sure it will be okay, I'd love to visit the lab."

"Great. It's a date." She winked.

Eric found it hard to be suspicious of her. She might just be dangling hope in front of him so that she could snatch it away, but he couldn't help but believe she was sincere. She seemed to have nothing but good intentions. He suspected that he might have been unfairly projecting his own feelings of guilt onto her. She reminded him so much of the woman he'd fallen for all those years ago, before he allowed his selfish ambitions to ruin what they had. He didn't regret the life that he and Katelyn had built, but he did regret having been so careless with Sharay's feelings and having hurt her so deeply.

****

Christopher called McIntyre to wish him and his wife, Cassie, a wonderful holiday and to express his appreciation for all that McIntyre had done for him and his family. It had been McIntyre who had taken Christopher under his wing when he was first elected to Congress and who had believed he'd make a fine running mate, despite objections from within their own party.

"How's he doing?" Tracy asked as she prepared for bed.

"Wonderful. He and Cassie plan to sleep late tomorrow."

"They can't. We have too much to do before …." She started to protest, but then realized that he was only teasing her. "Oh, that was evil. Well Mr. Vice President, now that we are alone, you can tell me what you would like me to do for you."

Christopher smiled as he pulled back the covers.

****

Cassie knew her husband better than anyone. She could tell when something was bothering him, and though he seemed happy, she knew something was wrong.

"What?" he asked, when he caught her watching him out the corner of his eye.

"Nothing."

"Good. I don't want you to worry about anything. This is going to be our last normal holiday season, with just the two of us, for a very long time, and I want us to fully enjoy ourselves. After I take office, we'll be surrounded, so no worrying or talk of politics at all for the next few days."

"That sounds great, but—"

He softly pressed a finger to her lips. "No 'buts.' That's an order."

"Okay, I'll agree to your demands on one condition. You have to follow your own decree."

"What are you talking about?"

"I see the concern in your eyes. I know something is wrong. What is it?"

"I'm not concerned. I was just mulling over my meeting with Senator Balile. He's asked to see me tomorrow, and I felt compelled to oblige."

"The election is over. I'm sure he just wants to put all the bad blood between you guys behind him. You have nothing to fear from him. He took his best shot, and you won. He has nothing to gain by coming after you now. I think he's a smart man. He has to know that it is in his best interest to put this rivalry to bed."

Everything in his spirit warned him that Balile was dangerous—and that the man was just getting started. Still, he didn't want to ruin the holiday for his wife. "I'm sure you're right," he told her.

"I am. The party backed you. You are their new golden boy. Even Balile has to respect that."

He forced an unconvincing smile. She didn't appear to notice.

****

Eric walked Sharay to her room before rushing to call Katelyn to tell her the wonderful news. Sharay watched the elevator doors close before she closed the door to her room.

"I'm surprised you didn't ask him to stay for a drink."

"He might wonder why you were here."

"Did he agree to return to Grayson?"

"He will," she assured Balile.

Chapter Twelve

Aaron quietly got out of bed. He did not want to wake Jennifer, but he needed to prepare for Sunday. He checked the clock. It was still very early, but he didn't mind getting up early—he couldn't sleep anyway. He had too much on his mind; he'd been lying awake in his bed for hours.

Since the inauguration ceremony, he'd received several invitations from churches all over the country. Though he'd never given much thought to becoming a pastor, an offer from a church in Virginia had definitely warranted consideration. They were offering him everything he didn't know he wanted, but he wasn't sure how Jennifer would react to the idea of relocating to Virginia.

Aaron peaked into his son's room before heading to the study. He loved to watch Justin sleep; it kept him grounded. When he watched his son, he remembered all the reasons he wanted to make the world a better place. He carefully put Justin's arm back under the blanket and pulled the covers over his toes.

"Good night, son," he whispered. He kissed his son's cheek softly before closing the door.

****

Katelyn helped Eric pack. She prided herself on being a strong, independent woman, but Talen's illness had shaken her very foundation. It had left her grasping for something or someone upon whom she could rely when desperation overwhelmed her, and Eric was that safe place.

She understood his decision to return to Grayson, and she agreed that she and Talen had to remain in New York. Grayson was their best chance to find a cure for their son, and since Eric had resigned his position at the lab, her surgical position at the hospital was the family's only reliable source of income and much-needed insurance. If they followed him to Colorado, there was no assurance that she'd be able to find a comparable position. Because of Talen's illness, private insurance wasn't an option. Intellectually, she understood and agreed with everything, but emotionally, she found things difficult to accept.

"I don't want you to worry. I'm going to come home every weekend, and I'll call every day. If anything goes wrong, I'll be on the next emergency flight back here. I know this is hard, but we can do this," he reassured her.

"I know. We'll be fine." She drew her lips into a tight smile.

Eric was not fooled, but still, he appreciated her attempt to make him feel better. "I know you will." He fastened his suitcase. "Remember, I'm only a phone call and one short layover away."

She hugged him good-bye.

Eric held her tightly. He never wanted to let go. He wasn't looking forward to moving back to Colorado. The life he led there seemed a lifetime ago. Katelyn and Talen were his life now. When he married Katelyn, he never looked back. He'd never even discussed Sharay, the baby, or his previous life in Colorado with her, and he didn't dare mention Sharay now. It was his burden alone to carry.

"Go. We'll be fine." She waved him off matter-of-factly.

He was grateful. He knew how hard this was for her. She'd be left to face each crisis alone. He kissed her tenderly before heading out the door. He saw Talen waving from his bedroom window, and it broke his heart. He wanted to rush back inside and find another way, but he knew that there was no other way. As he pulled away from the home they had built, he promised himself that it would not be for long.

****

Christopher and his speechwriter, Kelly Airs, were preparing for his next public appearance when the call came. He could not believe McIntyre was gone; he'd just spoken with him a day ago, and he had seemed so healthy. Christopher rushed to Cassie's side.

"I refuse to believe it was a heart attack," Cassie whispered.

"I know; I can't believe he's gone." Christopher patted her hand comfortingly.

"No. I mean I don't believe he died from natural causes. His heart was strong. This was no heart attack."

"What are you saying?" Christopher asked uneasily. "Did something happen to make you suspect foul play?"

"It's more about something he said. Did you know about his meetings with Senator Balile?"

"No, I didn't. I know they weren't the best of friends, but I'm sure the senator wouldn't—"

"He never trusted him. He felt ill every time he had to meet with him. You could tell it really upset him. He didn't like to discuss his meetings with the senator, but this time he did. He said if he allowed Balile to get his way, it would destroy everything he and this country stood for."

"Cassie, think about what you are suggesting. It's no secret that there was bad blood between him and Balile, but would the senator want him dead?"

"You weren't here when he came home. You didn't see his face. He was frightened."

"I don't want you to worry about anything, except taking care of yourself." Christopher felt sorry for her. He knew how difficult accepting the death of a loved one could be. As strained as his relationship with his father had been, Mitch's sudden death had sent him reeling. "I'll look into things. We'll get to the truth, no matter what it takes. We all loved him. The country has suffered an immense loss, and we all deserve answers, so put this out of your mind."

"Thanks. You meant so much to him. You were more than just his protégé. He loved you as if you were his own son. You have to find out what really happened. You are the only one I trust to do this."

"You can depend on me."

"I just know this has something to do with the research."

"What research?"

"You know Balile's been pushing for the expansion of stem-cell research and the lifting of the ban on human cloning, right?"

"Yes, of course."

"Well, after he met with the senator, he said that Balile had a problem with some of his policies. He said that Balile insisted that he back down concerning those policies that favored increased restrictions on the use of fetal material in stem-cell research." She lowered her voice to a whisper. "He said to do otherwise was to commit suicide."

"I'm sure that he meant political suicide." Christopher wished he knew what to say to her. He wanted to be supportive, but her accusations seemed far-fetched at best. He felt certain that they were the desperate rantings of a woman who'd just lost everything. She and McIntyre had been high school sweethearts. He'd never seen two people so much in love. He couldn't imagine losing his soul mate. His heart broke for her.

****

"How are you?" Sarah was happy to see Eric. She rarely got to see him since Talen's illness. She was happy that he had taken the time to see her on his way to the airport.

"Working hard."

"I know you are. It pains me to watch you and Katelyn working so hard. You have so little time to spend together. I wish there was something more I could do for you two."

"Trust me. Just being such a good friend helps."

"That goes without saying." Sarah smiled. "You know that you are the family that I wish I had had; after all, I did introduce the two of you."

"Thanks. There is something you can do for me. Katelyn spends almost all her free time taking care of Talen. I'm worried that she might get burned out. If you are ever out my way, would you stop in to see her? "

"I would be delighted to stop by the house and check in on her from time to time. Maybe I could watch Talen for her."

"I had better run, or I'll miss my flight."

"Have a safe trip."

"I will. I'll call you when I get back to Colorado." He hugged her.

"You'll be okay," she whispered into his ear.

Eric nodded. He didn't believe her, but he appreciated the sentiment.

****

Aaron expected that discussing his desire to accept the position as pastor of the Virginia church would be difficult, but what he didn't expect was the guilt he would feel. Jennifer had left New York right after graduation. She had never been very close to her family. Her father had abandoned her and her mother when she just a baby. He had not wanted children, so her mother blamed Jennifer. The decision to return to New York had been a difficult one, but since her return, she and her mother had begun to mend their troubled relationship.

"I understand how difficult this is for you. I know what I'm asking you to give up."

"I can paint anywhere, and I can still come back to show my work in the area galleries."

"That's not what I meant. You came back to New York because it was your home, and you've worked hard to lay down roots here. I would be asking you to give up the home you worked so hard to create."

"You and Justin are my home. My concern is that you may be taking on too many responsibilities. First there were the FLOCK elections, and then there were the protests and all the speaking engagements, not to mention your taking on more responsibilities at the church. I think you are spreading yourself too thin."

"I know how busy I've been lately, and you and Justin have been so patient. I promise that things are going to get better."

"How? When? Between the church and the FLOCK, what time do you possibly have to take on a position as the senior pastor of a church?"

"If I take the Virginia offer, I'll give up my position here, and reduce my commitments to the FLOCK"

"You'd do that? The organization means so much to you."

"I'd have no choice. Besides, I wouldn't be abandoning them. I'd stay involved, and I'd be leaving them in good hands."

Jennifer wanted to be supportive, but she couldn't help but worry. They saw so little of him already.

"I can do this, but only if I have your and Justin's support."

"I don't want to be selfish, but I don't want to become one of those successful couples who barely speak and don't know their own children."

"We could never be that couple. I'd give up everything before I allowed that to happen. I can do this. We can do this. I'm asking you to trust that I won't lose sight of my priorities."

"I do trust you." She softly kissed his eyelids. He pulled her into his arms. "You are my prince. I'd follow you anywhere."

Aaron held her tightly as they began to sway to a song that only they could hear.

"I love you," she whispered into his ear. She felt safe in his arms. She believed in him.

"I love you, too." He spun her around.

As relieved as Aaron was to have Jennifer's support, however, there was one more person whose approval he felt he needed.

The next morning, Aaron stood outside of Pastor Campbell's study. Next to telling his wife about his decision to leave, telling Pastor Campbell was the most difficult thing he had to do. When everyone else had discounted his decision to enter the ministry as a passing phase, it was Pastor Campbell who had taken him seriously and had counseled him in his decision. Though he did not need Pastor Campbell's permission to accept the Virginia offer, he did want his blessing.

Aaron knocked on the door.

"Come in, Aaron."

Aaron tentatively entered the study and sat across from his friend and mentor. He explained his decision to leave.

Campbell listened attentively as Aaron explained the pros and cons of his decision. He'd long seen the signs, and though it was always painful to watch one of your own leave, he knew that God had his hand on Aaron's life. He only hoped that Aaron was just as confident about this fact.

As Aaron continued to diagram the anatomy of his decision, explaining in detail each of the reasons he had for accepting or rejecting the offer, Campbell just listened and nodded. He waited until Aaron was finished.

"The main reason for not leaving would be because I'd be leaving a church that I consider my home," Aaron explained.

"I see," Campbell said.

Aaron was confused. He wasn't sure if Campbell was in agreement or not. "What does that mean? Do you think that I'm making a mistake?" Aaron could not believe that Pastor Campbell would not be happy for him.

"I didn't say that."

"Then what are you saying? Don't you think I'm ready? Don't you think I'd make a good pastor?"

"The question is, what do you think? Because I can't answer that question. It's not for me to say. I'm not the one who called you into the ministry in the first place. Only the one who called you can answer that question. I know that you can teach the word; I've heard you preach. I know you can lead; I've watched you with the children from the youth center. People believe in you. They'll follow you."

"But?" Aaron prompted him.

"The offer sounds quite wonderful, and I can see no logical reason not to take it, but the decision to become a pastor is never a logical choice; it's a spiritual one. For this reason, selecting a church has to be a spiritual one as well. It has to take more into account than just the foreseeable pros and cons. Have you prayed about this?"

"Of course I've prayed about this. I feel this is where God is leading me."

"Then you don't need a list, and you don't need my or anyone else's permission."

"I know, but I would like your blessing."

"You have that, and so much more. You have my respect and admiration. You have my prayers."

"That is all I've ever wanted."

"Then rejoice. This is an amazing journey you are about to undertake. It's not an easy one, but God never takes you to it without a plan to take you through it. Just remember that even a shepherd sometimes loses his way, so if you ever look around and need direction, look to the Master."

"I will," Aaron agreed.

"We're really going to miss you guys. Don't forget that this is your home. I fully expect you to bring your lovely family back to visit us often."

"Of course we will."

"Remember to keep your family and God first. Being a pastor can be a lonely job, so hold fast to the people who bring water to your desert."

Chapter Thirteen

Jennifer was determined to make a good impression on the church's congregation. She had always looked up to her pastor's wife, Trish, and over the years they had become the best of friends. Though Jennifer had been raised as a Christian, her family had only attended church on religious holidays, so she had been nervous about joining a church. She worried about how she would be received by the rest of the congregation, but Trish had reached out to her right away. Jennifer hoped the women of the congregation would come so see her as a friend and confidant.

They finally arrived at the church. Jennifer reached for a lint brush out of the car pocket. She ran it over the front of her skirt and down both sleeves. She wished she'd worn the pleated skirt instead.

"Stop fussing with your clothes. They're going to love you. How could they not?" Aaron tried to reassure her, but he could tell that she was still nervous.

The usher escorted Jennifer to her seat in the front. She held onto Justin's hand as if it were a lifeline. As she felt the congregation begin to warm up to her husband, she relaxed. Maybe he'd been right. Maybe she'd been worried for nothing.

After church, a parishioner asked to speak to Aaron in his office, so Jennifer waited in a chair just outside the choir room. She could hear the women singing as they changed out of their choir robes. She pulled Justin onto her lap and began to softly sing along with the women until he fell to sleep. After most of the women had gone, Jennifer thought she heard something else—her name. She strained so that she could better hear what was being said about her.

"Did you see what she was wearing?" one woman asked.

Jennifer did not recognize the voices of most of the women, but one of the voices sounded familiar.

"She's supposed to be some big-time artist in New York. I expected more."

"I didn't. I warned the board; now we're stuck with them," another woman added. Jennifer recognized the voice. It was Mrs. Maple. She was a direct descendant of the church's founding pastor and had been on the welcoming committee when they first arrived. Jennifer was heartbroken. She carried Justin to the car to wait for Aaron.

****

Senator Elroy's death from injuries he sustained in a recent car accident came as a surprise to Christopher. This was his third eulogy in nineteen months, first President McIntyre; then Justice Pike, from an apparent brain aneurism; and then Senator Elroy. Christopher was beginning to suspect that Cassie may not have been completely off base concerning Balile. Of those who had voiced the strongest opposition concerning stem-cell research, two had recently had an unexpected change of heart and three others were dead. Christopher was not sure whom he could trust, but he was certain that he had to quickly uncover Balile's connection. His life depended upon it.

Christopher glanced through the newspaper as he finished his morning coffee. He was disturbed to read that two young girls had gone missing, one not more than fifteen miles from where he had grown up. As upsetting as any child abduction was, what made these two abductions more disturbing were the mutilated animal remains found near the crime scenes. Even more disturbing was that both had taken place at almost the exact same time on opposite sides of the country. Recent investigations revealed similar cases all over the globe, dating back decades. Christopher tossed the newspaper on the table.

"What time will you be back?" Tracy asked.

"Late, but I'll call you from the office once I have a better idea," Christopher promised.

"How are things going with your investigation? Are you still having concerns about the senator?"

"Maybe I'm just seeing what I want to see, but Senator Elroy's death this soon after Supreme Court Justice Pike's death is a little too convenient."

"What are you saying? Is he responsible or not?"

He hesitated. He didn't want to worry her, but he couldn't lie to her either. "There's nothing definite to suggest foul play, but I know that before he died, McIntyre was concerned about Balile's secret connections to some group he called the Triad, and that Justice Pike and Senator Elroy were Balile's biggest obstacles to pushing this hearing."

"That is, except you."

"Yeah, except me. Look, don't worry. I'm keeping my eyes on the good senator." He tried to reassure her, but he knew that she had every reason to worry.

"What are you going to do about him? People around him are just dropping like flies. Who's to say you aren't next on his agenda?"

"I'm not sure what I can do at this time. You can't just order that a United States senator be investigated without legitimate evidence of wrongdoing. That is, unless you want to explain yourself to Congress."

"Have you said anything to Cassie yet?"

"No, not until I have something definite to tell her. I have a meeting with the senator tomorrow. He wants to discuss our country's stand on stem-cell research and our ban on cloning. Maybe then I'll have more to tell her. This is a very delicate matter. I have to proceed with caution."

"Please be careful. I don't want to lose you."

****

"Do we have someone in place?"

"Yes. Her name is Kelly Airs. She is one of our top students."

"Good. We may have to call upon her sooner than we thought."

"She will be ready."

"I have had an opportunity to check out some of the new recruits. They are quite impressive. I understand that retention rate is up from about 50 percent to about 80 percent. That is amazing. To what should I contribute the improved success rate?"

"New training techniques have been implemented that include the use of drug therapy."

"Are you telling me that they are high?"

"No, sir, Director, just controlled."

"Keep it that way. Junkies are of no use to us or to the master. This army must be ready and in place when they are called upon."

"They will be, sir."

"Good. Your life depends upon it."

****

"Hello Ms. Airs," Balile greeted the young woman.

She glanced uncomfortably around the hall to see if they were being watched. "What are you doing here?"

"I have a meeting with your boss," Balile answered. "I'm surprised you don't know that."

"He doesn't ask my permission every time he makes a move."

"Really? You must be slipping." He gently brushed his hand along her shoulder.

She pulled her arm away in disgust. "I'm doing my job," Kelly insisted. "He is coming around."

"In time for the vote?"

"He is very strong-willed, but I feel confident in my ability to help him see reason. Your being here can only complicate things."

"If the Triad felt confident in your ability to handle this situation alone, I would not be here, would I? Don't worry; we intend to offer the carrot before we resort to the stick."

"Won't that draw unwanted attention so soon after the death of President McIntyre? Is there no other way?" Kelly asked. She may not have been in love with Christopher, but she never wanted to see him in harm's way.

"The people will believe what they are told, just as long as their lives are not adversely affected. I'm sure it will be in their best interest to accept whatever we tell them. Besides, you read the papers, just like me. Either you're 100 percent for the Triad, or you're—"

"One hundred percent dead," Kelly completed the sentiment.

"Exactly." Balile knew that he did not have to explain to her the importance of following orders; she had grown up under Triad control since her abduction at age seven. "Nothing is final yet, but if the order is given, you are closest to him, and the honors will likely fall to you."

Balile was confident that if and when the time presented itself, she would perform as trained, but he did need to ensure that she did not lose her focus. She had been deep undercover for several years, and neither he nor the Triad was sure what effect that had had on her.

Balile started to explain further, but was interrupted by a young man, who informed him that the president was ready to meet with him. He escorted Balile to the Oval Office.

Christopher listened as Balile methodically explained the benefits of easing the restrictions, before explaining why he felt increased restrictions were necessary.

"It's unfortunate that there was no common ground we could reach on this matter," Balile smiled as he stood to leave.

"I don't see any, when your demands are both unreasonable and uncompromising. There is no way I can unilaterally lift the bans, nor would I want to at this time. We have an agreement with the international community."

"Your oath is to the welfare of the American people," Balile protested.

"Yes, and I'm sure that if made aware of the far-reaching implications of what you suggest, the American people would never agree to such drastic measures, even in these drastic times."

"Let me tell you something about the American people. The people will do what they have to do to ensure their own well-being. The American people have readily accepted every resolution introduced to them, moral or not, as long as it has benefited them personally, so let's not worry about 'the people.' They will accept whatever we tell them to accept." Balile crossed the room to stand over Christopher. Christopher remembered Cassie's words concerning Senator Balile. He tried not to show any visible signs of anxiety.

"I have to follow what I know in my heart is right, even if I stand alone." Christopher held his ground. "I will loosen the ban when I believe that we have fully investigated the dangers and the potentials for abuse."

"Who do you think you are? Those who oppose *me* rarely do so for long." Balile's smile was twisted.

"Is that a threat?"

"No, it's reality."

****

It was late when Aaron returned home. He had spent the entire afternoon at the church working on a speech to present at the next Board of Trustees meeting. Jennifer was waiting for him.

"Sorry I'm late. We were finalizing the speaker list for the anniversary," he explained as he sat across from her.

Out of the corner of his eye, Aaron caught sight of the medal on the coffee table. He was at once flooded by guilt as he remembered his promise to be at his son's competition.

Jennifer's expression didn't change. She wasn't angry, just disappointed.

"I'm so sorry. I completely forgot. Was he very disappointed?"

"What do you think? All the other fathers were there. He had told his friends that you would be there. He spent the entire time looking for you in the stands."

"I'll make it up to him."

"Don't bother." Jennifer closed the book that she had been reading and went to bed.

Aaron stood at Justin's bedroom door and watched him sleep. He had broken a promise to his son. Jennifer was right; he could not repair this with a simple apology. He needed to do better at balancing the responsibilities in his life. Aaron gently shook Justin awake.

"Hi, Daddy."

"I saw your medal. I'm really proud of you."

"Thanks."

"I'm sorry I missed it."

"It's okay."

"No, it's not. I should have been there. I didn't keep my word, but I will come to the next one. That's a promise. When is it?"

"Next month!" Excited, Justin sat up in the bed, beaming. "It's regionals!"

"That's perfect." Aaron hugged his son.

Aaron felt better. When he rose to leave, he was surprised to see Jennifer. She had been standing in the doorway, listening, and she didn't look pleased.

"I know that look." He brushed past her on his way to their bedroom. She followed. "What did I do now?"

"Don't make him promises you aren't prepared to keep. You'll just disappoint him again," Jennifer insisted.

"Look, I know I haven't been around much lately, but things are going to get better."

"They have to."

"I know I haven't given you any reason to believe this time will be any different." Aaron took his wife by the hand. "You know why I've been so busy. I just want to make the world a better place for him and for you. Is that so wrong?"

"I understand, but you can't expect him to understand. He's only a little boy." Jennifer shook her head and tried to pull her hand away, but Aaron gently pulled her into his arms. "You know I support your work. I know how important it is to you."

"Yes, and I know that I need to check my priorities. You don't have to say it."

"Yes, I do. I know how much you love the church, and there's nothing wrong with the FLOCK task force being one of your priorities. We're so very proud of your dedication. We just need to know that we are not at the bottom of the list of your priorities."

"Of course you aren't. You and Justin mean everything to me. We just need to spend more time together to reconnect with the important things in life, like our family and our marriage. I promise things are going to get better."

Jennifer smiled reluctantly. "What about the church's anniversary?"

"Don't you worry; everything is under control."

Jennifer playfully rolled her eyes at him.

Aaron sat on the foot of the bed and watched as Jennifer dressed for bed. She was as beautiful to him as the day they met. He loved her more than he could have ever imagined. She was a wonderful wife and mother, and he owed most of his accomplishments to her selflessness. Next to salvation, she was the best thing that had ever happened to him; and he knew that he didn't tell her that enough. Yes, he'd have to do a better job prioritizing.

"Where are you?" Jennifer smiled.

"What?"

"You look like you are a million miles away. Where were you?"

"Not too far away. I was just remembering when we were first married. Do you remember how we use to just hop into the car and ride all day?" Aaron softly ran his hand along the back of her hand.

"Yeah. I remember your faking car trouble just to give you an excuse to pull over to the side of the road to let the car 'rest.'"

"You knew that I was faking?"

"After the third or fourth time, I figured either we had to have the most unreliable car in the world, or you just wanted an excuse to hold me in your arms." Jennifer smiled wistfully. "I really miss that old car."

"I really miss those old trips." Aaron looked her directly in the eyes.

"That was a lifetime ago." Jennifer looked away. "We were just kids. We have far too many responsibilities now."

"Maybe that's our problem."

"What are you saying?"

"Maybe we can take a vacation to New York after the church's anniversary. I know how much you've been missing all our friends, and maybe you could schedule an appearance at a few of the galleries showing your paintings."

"Are you serious?" Jennifer's face lit up. Several of the New York galleries had been begging her to make an appearance, not to mention how much she was missing the Campbells. They had been like family to her.

"Make the arrangements. We'll make it a road trip."

Chapter Fourteen

Balile was aware of the bad blood between Sharay and her sister, Angela, and after having met Angela, he understood Sharay's contempt. She lacked Sharay's grace and style; in fact, he found that she had very little to offer at all, outside of her striking good looks and willingness to accommodate. Unfortunately, she was Neal's wife, which made her indispensable.

Balile had just received his orders from the Triad, and he had major plans for the team that required everyone to work together. He expected Sharay to put up the greatest resistance, so he planned to meet with her alone. He knew that he would be asking a lot from her, and he wanted to give her an opportunity to come to terms with not only having to work with her sister but with Neal as well.

Balile wasn't sure how she would respond to the news that Neal had faked his own death and that Angela had been aware of it for years. He expected her to be shocked and confused, but he feared that she might also feel that her trust had been betrayed by him as well. She was an intricate part of the Triad's plans, and if she lost faith in him, it could pose a huge problem. Any delays could put the success of the plan as a whole in jeopardy, which could not be permitted. He hoped that her ambition would be enough to suppress her suspicion, but first things first—the feud between the sisters had to end.

Balile arrived early to the hotel restaurant where he planned to meet Sharay for dinner to discuss things. When he saw her arrive, he checked his watch. He smiled; she was early. He had hoped she'd be on time, and as usual, she did not disappoint. The hostess led Sharay to Balile's table. He rose to greet her.

"It is so good to see you again. I was surprised to hear from you so soon. When my husband told me that you had already arranged for me to testify before Congress about the benefits of stem-cell research in a few months, I was floored. We've been trying to get a hearing on the subject for years, but because it's such a controversial topic, no one has wanted to take a stand one way or the other." Sharay had not expected him to be able to make progress so quickly. She was impressed.

"When I make a promise, I keep it."

"Remind me to never doubt you again." She laughed.

"I'll do that." He ordered their drinks. "I'm happy to keep up my end of the bargain. Now, however, it's your turn to do something for us."

"I'll do anything you need me to do."

"I hope you mean that. When we first met, I asked you if you were serious about your craft. You said you were."

"I did and I am. This is my life's work. It means everything to me, and I also keep my promises. There is nothing that I wouldn't do for the success of the project."

"Good, because I want you to know that I've invited your sister and her husband to join us later."

Sharay felt herself stiffen but caught herself and recovered quickly. She'd become quite adept at hiding her emotions.

"It's okay. I know about the tension between you and your sister. That's why I asked you here. I thought we could talk."

"About?"

"We should talk about what we should expect from each other." He folded his napkin and sat back in his chair. "I don't want there to be any misunderstanding between us. I need for us to be on the same page concerning this matter. I have given you my full commitment and the commitment of those I represent to back your research, but make no mistake—we expect the same commitment from you that you should expect from us."

"Of course you should, and I've done everything you've asked. You said the project needed Eric, so I swallowed my pride, and I delivered Eric. You said I should get close to him. Well, I think we both can agree that we've gotten very, very close." Her tone, though controlled, was defiant.

"We have no problems with anything you've done so far, but you do seem more than a little concerned about my decision to involve Angela and her husband. As I said, I know that there has been bad blood between you and your sister, but you have to trust me. We're on your side. We all want the same thing. You need us, and we need her—or actually, her husband. It's as simple as that."

"I just feel a little blindsided. I can't imagine what my sister or her husband can possibly have to do with my research. My sister has no scientific background at all, and I know most of the scientists in this field, and I'm sure that I've never met her husband." Sharay hadn't been aware that Balile even knew her sister, and she didn't appreciate finding out like this, but it was becoming increasingly obvious to her that there was a lot that she didn't know about the senator and the group that he represented. She wasn't sure what she had gotten herself into, but if he could deliver on his promises, she was prepared to work with Satan himself.

"I'm not asking you to accept what I'm saying on blind faith. I'm more than willing to explain, but their involvement is non-negotiable."

"Is he a scientist?"

"No, but his involvement is pertinent to the success of this project. I think you'll understand once you meet him. As far as how you feel about your sister, that is your own business. I've met the woman, and frankly I don't blame you for despising her. After we've accomplished our task, you never have to see her again, but until she and her husband have exhausted their usefulness, you had better become the best of buddies. If that's asking too much, then I expect you ladies to fake it. Do you understand?"

She half-heartedly nodded.

"We've invested a lot time and money in you and your team. We've put all of our faith in your ability and commitment to making this work. If we have the wrong person, you need to let me know now before we go any further." He knew that she'd never pass up the chance to fulfill her lifelong ambition.

"No. You have the right person. I'm sure Angela and I can put our differences aside for the good of the team."

"Good, I'm glad that that has been resolved." He needed her to understand that Triad business took precedence over everything else, and he felt confident that she did.

"Hello, Senator," Angela greeted him as she approached their table. "It's wonderful to see you again, Sharay. It's been too long."

"Is Neal waiting?" Balile got straight to the point.

"Yes. He's upstairs in room 365."

"I'm sure you ladies can behave yourselves for a little while. Join us in thirty minutes. I want a few moments alone with Neal."

"I'm sure we can find something to talk about." Angela winked at her sister.

"Play nice," Balile warned her before leaving.

"So, how does it feel, being back with Eric?" Angela gloated. She knew that this was a sore topic for her sister, and she was not about to miss a chance to rub her nose in it.

"It feels like a lie."

"Then why not just enjoy the fantasy. You've got him back, at least until Talen gets well. That is, *if* he gets well."

"What's that suppose to mean?" Sharay didn't like what Angela was implying.

"I just don't think his well-being factors into any of this. They want him alive, that's for sure, but no one said anything about wanting him well."

"I'm not stupid. I know all this isn't about saving one little boy, but you sound like there's a conspiracy to keep him sick."

"Let's just say, the world as you know it is about to get turned upside-down. But keep heart, little sister, if you play your cards right, you may end up with everything you've ever wanted."

"How would you know what I want?"

"I know more than you think. I know about the abortion you had when you and Eric were still together; I know that your husband believes that you're trying to get pregnant, but that you're really still on the Pill; and I know that you're still in love with your ex. Have I missed anything?" Angela checked her watch. "Let's go."

"It hasn't even been twenty minuets yet."

"It is better to arrive early rather than late. Balile hates it when you're late." She led Sharay to the elevator.

"You seem to know a lot about Senator Balile. I wonder how your husband feels about that."

"My husband wouldn't have it any other way. He encourages our closeness. He believes in Senator Balile completely, so if the senator happens to have an itch that needs to be scratched, my husband considers it an honor to have me help him scratch it."

"You must be so proud." Sharay almost felt sorry for Angela.

"Don't patronize me. At least my husband sees the big picture, and I don't have to lie to him about what I do."

"Maybe that's because he doesn't care about what you do."

"I hear that you and Eric have gotten very close. I wonder if your husband is as understanding."

"We're discreet."

"Are you telling me that your husband doesn't have a clue? Of course he does, but he also knows how talented Eric is. He recognizes the benefits of having someone of his caliber working at the lab. Why else would he have allowed you to bring Eric back to Grayson? Either he's an idiot, or he has to know that you're sleeping with Eric. He closes his eyes and pretends to believe in your fidelity. Your husband understands the big picture, just as well as mine does. Mine is just man enough to own up to it."

"Is that why I'm here? Am I going to learn what the 'big picture' is?" Her tone was icy. The elevator door opened to the third floor.

As they approached the room, Angela suddenly became quite serious. She paused outside the hotel room door. Sharay could tell that she was afraid.

"The senator can be charming at times, but he is no one to take for granted," Angela warned. She stroked a small scar at the base of her neck. "If provoked, he can be as ruthless as he is driven. If you know what is good for you, you'll remember that. He likes you, but don't get in his way. He's all about the big picture, so just pray that he never decides that you no longer fit into that picture."

Sharay wondered about the scar, but thought it better not to ask. She knew that Angela had always prided herself on her flawless good looks, and she wasn't sure she wanted to know what had happened.

"Look, we both have a lot to gain, and even more to lose. I say we call a truce." Angela offered Sharay her hand.

"Do you really think that we could become friends?" Sharay asked in earnest. Something or someone must have really frightened Angela for her to be offering a truce.

"No, but we could become allies. I know that it's hard for you to trust me, but you could always trust me to do what was best for me. You're an intricate part of the senator's vision for the future. You're his golden child, so in destroying you, I'd only be hurting myself."

Sharay nodded. For the first time in their lives, the sisters were of one accord. When they entered the room, Neal and Balile were still discussing matters.

"Have you given much thought to what I should tell him? I think he's going to expect a substantial explanation," Neal protested. Though he trusted Balile completely, he wasn't sure his suggestion that they tell Eric that he was still alive after all these years was a good one. "We were extremely close, and I'm sure he's going to feel betrayed. We can't predict how he'll react. We're so close to the finish line. Do we dare risk it? What can I possibly say that will explain what we've done to him?"

"Tell him the truth."

"The truth?" Neal was taken off guard. Admitting to faking his own death was one thing, but confessing to killing their father was another.

Balile held up a hand to silence him when he noticed that Angela and Sharay had entered the room. "You're just in time. I'm glad to see that you didn't kill each other."

"We came to an agreement." Sharay winked at Angela. "You must be Angela's husband. It's wonderful to meet you." She extended her hand.

"Thanks. I'm delighted to finally meet you as well. I'm Eric's brother, Neal."

Sharay never felt her legs weaken beneath her as she fainted. Neal caught her, and helped her to the couch.

"Grab me a wet cloth," Neal instructed Angela.

"Is she okay?"

"She's fine." Neal wiped Sharay's forehead as she awakened.

She pulled away.

"Relax. You're safe here." Neal tried to calm the frightened woman.

"You're supposed to be dead." Sharay felt her mind spiraling as she tried to grasp what was happening.

"How do they say it? Rumors of my death have been greatly exaggerated." He laughed. "I'll explain later. Right now, there are more important things to handle."

Angela handed Sharay a drink to calm her nerves. She downed the drink quickly. She listened as Balile explained the Triad's vision and the roles they were all to play.

"If you play your cards right, we'll all come out ahead," Angela promised.

"I just don't want to hurt anyone, least of all Eric. Maybe I'm the idiot, but I still care for him." Sharay could only imagine the worst.

"We've gone too far. There's no turning back." Angela held her sister's hand comfortingly.

"You are the only one who can protect him. You're not doing this to him; you're doing this for him. No one is going to get hurt," Neal promised, "at least, no one who matters."

****

Marcus tried not to notice the whispers of those around him. He knew that they were all discussing him and his miraculous return. He felt his mother squeeze his hand reassuringly and found it surprisingly comforting. He was amazed at how readily she had accepted him into her life and heart. Though he barely remembered her, she had obviously never forgotten him. Her love for him was unconditional.

He sat with his eyes focused on the speaker. She wasn't that much older than he was. She was quite passionate about what she was saying, but he was more interested in her as a woman than as an activist. He found her slightly less slender curves extremely attractive. He wondered if he would get the opportunity to get to know her while he was there.

"Those who argue the benefit of stem-cell research accuse us of putting our beliefs in front of human rights. I would argue that it is our belief in the rights of all humans that sets us apart. Unlike our adversaries, we are not willing to create life just to destroy it, or to sacrifice the very youngest of us to benefit the rest of us." Kira's words embodied the very essence of the FLOCK's values. As the guest speaker and longtime board member, she recognized the importance of these rallies. It was important to keep the members focused and motivated.

Marcus glanced around the room. He wondered if any of them had a clue what was going to happen. He suspected that they all believed they knew the face of evil, but he knew differently. He knew that until they had stared into the face of the Triad, they would never know true evil, not like the evil that was about to be unleashed upon the group.

After concluding her motivational speech, Kira returned control of the podium to Scott Allen, the president of the FLOCK, to close out the meeting.

"Before we adjourn, I'd like you all to rejoice with my wife, Mary and me. As anyone who knows us knows, our son was taken from us, years ago, and though our faith in God's love has never wavered, the return of our son after so many years is more than we could have hoped for. Will everyone please join us in welcoming our long-lost son, Marcus." Scott's voice cracked. "Praise the Lord."

"Halleluiah!" someone yelled.

"Amen!" echoed another.

"To God be the glory!" Scott concluded the meeting.

"Forever, amen," the group chimed in unison.

As Marcus and his parents walked to the parking lot, Marcus asked about Kira. Scott smiled. He recognized that Kira was a little older than Marcus, but she was a strong woman of faith, and he could do a whole lot worse.

****

Sharay stood silently in Eric's doorway as she'd done so many times before, watching as he waited for the results to yet another test. She had watched for months as his confidence shrank, and his frustration grew with each failed result. Despite all the pain he had caused her and her own better judgment, she still loved him, and it broke her heart to watch him struggle in vain. Though she realized that he would leave her the moment he found the answers he needed, Sharay wanted to help him more than anything.

"How's it going? Trying to get one last test in before you head home for the weekend?"

"Things could be better, but you know me. I won't give up so long as there's breath in my body, or at least in my son's body." He knew how morbid he sounded, but he lacked the strength to keep up the pretense.

"You're giving this all you have. What else can anyone ask from you?"

"Success."

"We don't control that."

"Then who does?"

"I wish I knew. All you can do is to keep trying." She wanted so much to tell him about Neal, if for no other reason, than to give him a reason to hope.

"What's this about? Just say it. Have you given up on me so soon, or is the lab just moving in another direction?"

"Neither. I could never give up on you. You are one of the most brilliant men I've ever met, and when I said that the lab would fully back your research, I meant that, too. I'm just saying you should give yourself a break."

Eric knew that she was right, but he'd already committed too much and paid too high of a price. He'd sacrificed what might be his son's final days, precious moments that he could never get back. He could accept nothing less from himself than finding a cure.

"Then what is this all about?" he asked, but he wasn't sure if he really wanted to know the answer.

"I have no doubt that you'll find a cure, but you said it yourself. Talen didn't look good the last time you left. What if it's too late? What if you find the cure, but it's just not in time?"

"It has to be."

"But what if it's not?"

Eric dropped his pen on his desk. What Sharay suggested was the unthinkable. He had not allowed himself to even contemplate the concept.

"What if I had an answer to your most pressing problem?"

Eric sat up in his chair. He knew her too well to think that her words were idle ramblings. She had his full and undivided attention.

"What if I could buy you more time?"

"How much time?"

"An entire lifetime."

"What's that supposed to mean?"

"We've done it. We've cloned a human embryo."

Eric could not believe what he was hearing.

"We didn't actually bring it to term, but we could have. I swore to my husband that I would not bring an embryo to term until we finally got the go ahead from congress, but that's the only thing delaying us."

Eric could not hide his shock. He wasn't sure how he felt about what she was saying.

"Don't look at me that way. Don't think that every other lab is not doing the same thing, but that's not why I'm telling you this."

"You're not suggesting what I think you're suggesting."

"We'll do it together, and no one has to know."

"What are you saying?" He grasped her by her shoulders. "What about the ban?"

"What about your son? I see how desperate you are to save him, and though you are a brilliant mind, you are not God. Given enough time, I have no doubt that you could find the cure to anything, but time is not a luxury you have."

"The law expressly—"

"The law of the jungle always trumps man's arbitrary laws. Why should some congressman who's never even met your child get a say in what you do to save him. You have a right to save your son by any means necessary."

"This is insane! What you suggest is impossible!"

"Why? Why is it impossible?"

"It wouldn't be him."

"Of course it would be him, every single DNA strand."

"He'd have no memory of his life."

"No, but he'd be alive. We're just giving him an opportunity to live the life that has been so cruelly stolen from him. I'm not saying give up on Talen. I'm just saying have a backup plan in case things don't go your way." She took Eric's hand in hers.

Eric snatched his hand away. "However good our intentions may be, we can't control where this technology will lead. Once we turn this corner, there is no going back. We do this, and we could be opening up a Pandora's Box."

"I say we smash that box to hell. I care about the ethical issues that will face the future as a result of our actions just as much as everyone else does, but I care more about those who are suffering right now."

"Lower your voice. Someone might hear you." Eric still could not believe what she was saying. He didn't know what concerned him more, that her suggestions were radical or that they were beginning to make sense to him.

"If you ask me, those conservative human rights do-gooders are the real hypocrites. They say they stand for human life, but then they block the very research that could improve the quality of that life for millions." Sharay did not try to hide her contempt.

What Sharay was suggesting, even if successful, could not only cost them both their careers but their freedom as well. Eric understood better than anyone the danger of what she was suggesting, but more than that, he understood the ramification of not doing it. He relented, and Sharay explained to him what he had to do.

"I will need a sample of his DNA." She pressed a small collection kit into his hand.

****

"The lobbyists have really been snapping at my heels as of late," Christopher complained.

"Then maybe you need to throw them a bone." Kelly didn't try to hide her contempt for his ethics.

"I'm not going to give in to their pressure."

"Really? Not even to preserve your standing in the poll?"

"Not even to save my career. I've made so many mistakes, but this is too important. I don't want this to be my legacy."

"Aren't you being a little dramatic?" Kelly's tone was harsh and cold.

It was obvious to Christopher how distant she'd become. He hoped it was just the stress, but he suspected there was more.

"It's not the kind of world I want to leave to my child," Christopher insisted.

"Oh, I know exactly what you mean. Who would want to live in a world without sickness or disease? Yeah, I really can see why you're so torn."

"Now who's being a little dramatic? This is not the answer to world peace."

"How do you know that?" Kelly snapped.

"I don't need this right now, not from you, too."

"I've got to go."

"I thought you were staying the night."

"I guess I don't need that right now from you, either." Kelly stormed out of the room. Time was running out, and she was getting desperate.

****

Marcus helped his father load the car after the meeting, but he did not return home with his parents. He told them that he was meeting friends at a local diner. Scott offered to give him a ride, but Marcus explained that he would rather walk to give himself a chance to clear his head before hooking up with his friends. Scott reluctantly conceded, and he and Mary returned home without their son.

Marcus watched as his parents drove away, then he rushed to catch up with Kira. "Hi."

"Hello, Marcus. I didn't get the chance to officially welcome you home, but we are all so happy for you and your family. We all love your parents. They are truly wonderful people. I was very young when you disappeared, but I remember how sad they were."

"I'm glad that they had you all to help them through it."

"It was our pleasure."

"I don't see your car, "he said. "Are you walking back to the hotel?"

"Yes, I'm only staying a few blocks from here." She smiled.

"May I walk with you?"

"That would be wonderful."

As Marcus walked Kira back to her hotel, he imagined that they were no different from any other young couple trying to get to know each other better.

"Do you really believe everything you said tonight? You believe that a clump of cells smaller than this cell phone should have the same rights as you and me?"

"Of course I do. Don't you?"

"Do I have to?"

"The only thing you have to do is keep an open mind. Give us a chance to explain why we feel so strongly about protecting the rights of those without a voice."

"I can do that."

"This is where I say good night." Kira stopped in front of the hotel.

Marcus leaned in to kiss her on the lips, but Kira turned and offered him her cheek.

"Good night, Marcus." She smiled as she closed the door.

Marcus thought about all that she had said and all that he had heard at the meeting. He was surprised at just how passionate they all were in their beliefs. He had always been taught that Christians were no better than superstitious fools, with their feet planted two thousand years in the past and their heads floating in the clouds. They were not what he had expected. She was not what he expected.

Several blocks later, Marcus found himself standing in front of the small diner where he was to meet his contact. He glanced into the window. He was relieved to find it empty, except for an older couple sitting in a corner booth. He decided not to wait. He would just explain that they must have just missed each other. As Marcus turned to leave, he felt a tight grip on his shoulder. It startled him, and he shivered as though his blood had suddenly run cold.

"Were you leaving?" Neal asked the young man.

"No, I was just looking for you."

"Well, then, I guess it's a good thing that you found me, or should I say, we found each other." Neal led Marcus into the diner.

****

Tracy lay in bed, staring at the empty space beside her. She knew when she married Christopher that there would be many nights when duty called him from her side, but instinct warned of something more. There was nothing specific, just several little things that did not add up. She felt uneasy; the knots in her stomach made it impossible for her to sleep.

She heard the door open, but pretended to be asleep. She knew that she and Christopher would have to deal with her suspicions, but on her terms and not tonight.

"Tracy," Christopher whispered. There was no answer. He was grateful. He had completely lost track of time, and he wasn't prepared for a confrontation.

Christopher quietly undressed and gently slipped into the bed beside her. As he stared up at the ceiling, he wondered what he was doing. He loved his wife and child, but he couldn't seem to get Kelly out of his system.

Christopher knew that he was being reckless, but what frightened him most was that he didn't care. He wasn't sure if he had feelings for Kelly or if it was just the thrill of being with her. Either way, he knew that he was risking too much. Though she hadn't said a word, he was sure that Tracy was beginning to suspect that there was something between them, and he wasn't sure if his career or his marriage could rebound.

Chapter Fifteen

Katelyn grabbed the phone on the first ring. It had been raining all night, and Eric was late.

"Hello?"

"Hi, sweetie. It's me."

"Where are you, honey?"

"The weather caused my flight to be late," Eric explained.

"I hate your traveling in this weather. Please be careful getting home. Talen will still be awake when you get here," Katelyn reassured him.

"You don't have to do that," he insisted.

"It's not me. You know that there is no way Talen is going to sleep before his daddy gets home."

"I know." Eric smiled to himself. "Tell Talen I'll be home soon and that I'm bringing him a present."

"You didn't," Katelyn whispered.

"I promised him a dog when he got older. Tomorrow he'll be ten, and hitting double digits is a big moment in a boy's life."

"Yes, I know. I suppose it's an important moment in his father's life as well." Katelyn laughed.

"I love your laugh. I really miss it." Eric bit into his lower lip. There were so many things he wanted to say to her, but nothing seemed right. He stroked the puppy on the seat beside him.

"He's going to be so excited." She knew that they had planned to wait until Talen was older and better prepared for the responsibilities associated with raising a puppy, but she understood Eric's reluctance to wait.

"Yeah. Don't tell him, though. I really want to see his face when he finds out that he's getting a dog for his birthday."

"Of course I won't. This is your surprise," Katelyn promised. "See you soon. Be safe."

"I promise." Eric placed his cell phone on the car seat beside him without taking his eyes off his son's bedroom window. He willed himself to move. How could he go inside? The only thing harder than leaving Talen each Sunday, was facing him empty-handed each Friday, and though the puppy was a wonderful gift, it was not the gift they needed. Eric knew that he'd eventually have to face his family. He couldn't stay in the car forever. Eventually, one of his concerned neighbors would notice and call the police, or worse, his wife would recognize his car.

****

Aaron paced back and forth as he chose his words carefully. He loved the way the old floorboards creaked under his weight. He'd found that the creak helped him with his timing. He closed his eyes as he visualized his congregation.

"The steps of a righteous man ..."

"Excuse me, Pastor Drake," a raspy voice interrupted.

Aaron turned to see the church's choir director Mrs. Maple standing behind him.

"Yes, Sister Maple, what can I do for you?" Aaron didn't like being interrupted, but he knew that Mrs. Maple was not someone he should or could let wait. As a direct descendant of the church's founding pastor, Mrs. Maple was the most influential person at the church.

"The choir is finished."

"Great, I'll just be a few moments more. I'll be sure to lock up before I leave." Aaron checked his watch. It was much later than he had thought.

"I've been told that you've been invited to testify before Congress next month."

"Yes. The entire task force has fought extremely hard for this opportunity, and I was selected to speak for the group. I consider it a real honor."

"I'm sure you do." Her tone was slightly more condescending than usual, a fact not lost on Aaron. "I suppose being good friends with the president doesn't hurt either."

"Was there anything else you needed?"

"This year is the church's two hundredth anniversary."

"Of course, we are all very excited about the celebration. I hope you aren't worried about my trip. I'll only be gone for a few days and I'll be back well before the celebration. Jennifer will be staying behind, so if you need anything, you can give her a call."

"Yes." She pursed her lips. "Well, actually, that is what I wanted to talk to you about."

"I don't understand."

"I was meeting with some of the sisters of the church."

"I wasn't aware that a meeting had been called."

"It wasn't that kind of meeting. Some of the sisters and I meet once a month for tea to discuss church affairs. Many of the sisters have voiced their concerns to me—they feel your wife may not have fully grasped the significance of this immense occasion."

"Some of the sisters, huh? I assure you, my wife is just as excited about this anniversary as I am."

"That may be, but as my late father and grandfather were so fond of saying, 'a man or woman is judged by his or her actions.'" She lovingly caressed the podium. She didn't care who this new pastor was supposed to be; it was her duty to make sure he provided her family's church with the leadership it deserved.

"Maybe you should just say what it is you came to tell me." Aaron had long since grown weary of the cat-and-mouse games that Mrs. Maple played. He hated the hypocritical way she enforced her own brand of morality through demands thinly disguised as suggestions and criticisms disguised as expressions of concern.

After Mrs. Maple's father died without naming his successor, the trustee board had invited Aaron to take over as pastor. He could only imagine how difficult it must have been for her to watch a stranger become pastor of the church that had been pastored by a member of her family since its inception, almost two hundred years ago, but he had had enough.

"Being a pastor's wife is a difficult calling, at best, and the good Lord knows that not every woman is so called," she continued.

"If you're finished, I really must return to my work." He turned to leave. There was no way he was going to stand there and be lectured to by this pompous hypocrite. "I'll be sure to give Jennifer your best."

"As I was saying, a tree is judged by its fruit, and a pastor's family is his first fruit. Jennifer may or may not have been called, but either way, she is a pastor's wife. There are duties and responsibilities that are expected of her."

Aaron bit his lip to keep form screaming at the woman's audacity. He shot her a stern look.

"It's time for her to step up and assume her role as this church's first lady—she should fake it, if necessary." She'd warned the board of trustees against selecting such a controversial pastor with such a young family, but they'd been wooed by his superstar status.

Aaron could taste the slight saltiness of the blood trickling from the corner of his lip.

"You're bleeding. Are you okay?"

"Yes, I just bit my lip." Aaron wiped the blood from his mouth.

"It happens." She smiled. Checkmate. "Well, I've taken up enough of your time. I'll let you rehearse. We wouldn't want to disappoint the entire congregation, would we?"

****

Eric paused outside the door. He felt the cool rain as it soaked his face. He was grateful for the rain. He rang the bell.

Katelyn was startled awake by the doorbell. She hadn't intended to fall asleep. She must have been more exhausted than she had realized. She straightened her clothes and pasted on a smile as she opened the door.

"I'm so happy you're finally home. How was the drive? Were the roads very bad?"

"I wouldn't say bad, just very wet." Eric forced a smile before looking away.

"You better take off that wet coat before you catch your death."

"How is he?" Eric finally gathered the strength to ask.

"The same, but now that you're home, I'm sure he's going to feel so much better."

"You know, this never gets any easier."

"You can't let him see you looking worried."

"I know. I know." Eric squeezed her hand reassuringly. "I was just saying that this never gets any easier. I hate being away from him so much, especially now."

"He knows, but he also knows how hard you are working to find a cure."

"What if I can't?"

"You will."

"But what if I can't?"

"Let's not do this. Go see your son. He's been waiting for you all night. Go ahead. Take him his present." Katelyn watched as her husband climbed the stairs to their son's bedroom with the puppy tucked under his shirt.

****

Late that night, an envelope addressed to Tracy lay on the night table of the bedroom. Both she and Christopher tried to ignore the elephant in the room, but the pale manila envelope could not have been more imposing if it had been bright red with neon lights. Christopher watched as Tracy packed her belongings into the matching luggage they had been given as a wedding gift.

"What are you doing? This is really getting old," he insisted.

Tracy meticulously folded a nightgown before placing it into a suitcase.

"You know that you're not leaving, so why are you putting us through all of this drama?"

She zipped the suitcase and added it to the several others just outside the bedroom door.

"Don't do this. You know that I was set up."

Tracy shot him an angry glare. He may not have sent her the pictures, but no one tricked him into cheating on her.

"You have to know I never meant for any of this to happen," he apologized.

"What did you want to happen? Half those shots were taken here at the White House. You weren't even trying to be discreet. How do you think that makes me feel?"

"I've apologized. What more can I do?"

Tracy snatched her robe from behind the door and jammed it into a small overnight bag.

"We are not finished. We have to deal with this; we have to talk things out. We have too much invested in this relationship to give up so easily. You can't just run away from this."

"Maybe not, but I need time." Tracy felt sick as she remembered the pictures. "I can forgive a lot of things. The Lord only knows how much I have had to forgive, but I can't forgive this. I'll call you as soon as we arrive."

****

Aaron pulled into his driveway. He was exhausted. There was so much to do before his trip to Washington DC; he wasn't sure how he was going to do it all. Not only did he need to prepare to testify before Congress, but he also had to get ready for the church's anniversary, all while managing his regular duties as a pastor, husband, and father.

Aaron turned off the ignition. He wasn't ready to go inside just yet. He hoped everyone would be asleep—he was in no mood for "small talk." His argument with Mrs. Maple could not have come at a more inopportune time. It had left him emotionally drained, and now on top of everything else he had to do, he had to decide how to handle the "sisters" and their secret meetings. Aaron knew that weeds left unchecked could destroy even the best kept garden.

As he opened the door, he saw that all the lights had been turned off. He listened for the television; there was nothing. He breathed a sigh of relief and headed upstairs to bed.

As he passed the dining room, he peaked inside. A sudden wave of guilt swept over him, as the faint smell of roast beef greeted him, and he saw the table set with the good china and a floral centerpiece. He had forgotten his promise. He had missed so many family dinners over the last few months, and Jennifer had been so patient.

Aaron quietly dressed for bed and gently slid next to Jennifer. She stirred slightly. He was careful not to wake her. He kissed her softly before rolling over and going to sleep. He promised himself that as soon as things calmed down, he'd make things up to her.

Chapter Sixteen

Vice President Victor Mitchell relaxed with a book as he took a sip of his piping hot coffee. It didn't get any better than this. His wife, LeeAnn, was attending a benefit, and he had the entire house to himself, or at least, almost entirely to himself. Mitchell smiled, and looked up from his book as he noticed his assistant approaching with a man.

"Hello, Mitchell. It's good of you to see me on such short notice." Senator Balile offered his hand.

"That'll be all, Kyle. I'll let you know when my guest is ready to leave."

"Yes Vice President Mitchell."

"He's yummy." Balile smiled.

"Get to the point. What's this about? I thought we agreed to be discreet."

"He looks younger than I expected. How old is he? Twenty-one? Nineteen?"

"Let it drop, Balile. I'm not entirely comfortable with your coming to my home this way."

"Would you have rather me come to your office?"

"I'd rather you get to the point."

"Well, then, let's dispense with decorum."

"Let's."

"You made a commitment to me and my supporters. We don't feel that you've been living up to your end of the bargain," Balile said.

"Well, I guess that's just too bad."

"Yes, too bad for you. We've invested a lot of money, and worse, a lot of time on this endeavor. We will not accept anything short of your full commitment." Balile removed an envelope from his pocket and handed it to

Mitchell. "You see, we all have our skeletons. It's all about knowing which closets to open."

"I will not be threatened." Mitchell held his ground.

"No threat intended. I just wanted you to know that these pictures existed. We're your friends, and as your friends, we are fully committed to protecting your interests, and I am sure you are just as committed to furthering ours."

"You're my friends? Well, I suppose you just stumbled upon these pictures, huh?"

"Yes, I did, and there were several other shots, too, but they were not in as good taste as these. It's not really my taste, but I can see what you see in him. I think you should be happy that I was the one who found out about this, and not those vultures who hide behind their right to freedom of the press."

Mitchell held out the pictures to Senator Balile, but Balile refused the envelope.

"No. You keep those. They're for your scrapbook. Can I tell my supporters that you are fully on board?"

"I always was."

"Great. I told them not to worry. I knew you were a man of your word." Balile clapped Mitchell on the back. "I'll find my own way out. Maybe I'll run into that cute little assistant of yours."

Mitchell crushed the envelope, as he watched Balile walk away.

"Kyle!"

Kyle rushed to Mitchell's side. "Yes, sir. Is there anything wrong?"

"I'll be joining my wife for lunch. Will you make the arrangements?"

"Today? I thought we were—"

Mitchell held out his hand to stop him. "Will that be a problem?"

"No. I'll make the arrangements and notify your wife."

Mitchell collapsed into his chair, which only moments ago had held such comfort. Balile had him just where he wanted him, and there was nothing he could do about it. Even if he had wanted to back out of his deal with Balile and support the president, there was no way he could do that now. He'd sold his soul for power, only to realize too late that it all was an illusion. He was a puppet and Balile was the puppeteer.

****

"Have you heard from Vice President Mitchell?" Christopher asked Nancy, his personal secretary.

"No, sir, Mr. President. The vice president has not checked into the office this morning. No one has spoken to him all day. Should I try him on his cell phone?"

"Do whatever it takes, but get him on the phone."

"Yes, sir, and by the way, Ms. Kelly Airs is waiting for you in your office."

"Thank you, Nancy. She must be here about the press conference."

"Whatever you say," Nancy mumbled, hiding her disgust.

After having served several political officials over the last thirty-two years, Nancy had seen her share of opportunistic vultures, the kind of people who gravitated to the wealthy and the powerful. She had no respect for women who allowed wives to do all the hard work while they reaped the rewards, and Ms. Kelly Airs was one of the worst she'd seen.

"Long night?" Kelly teased as Christopher sat in a chair directly across from her.

"You should know." Christopher tossed the newspaper on the desk. The front page showed a photo of him kissing an unidentified woman.

"What? I know you are not blaming me for this. There are two of us in that picture." She pushed the newspaper back toward him.

He looked away.

"Look, I'm sorry if I'm being snide, but you had to see this coming, so why are you acting like a victim?" Kelly's tone softened.

"This is my career. Can you understand that?"

"No, of course not. I guess you're the only one suffering here. Did you once stop to think what this could do to my credibility if I'm identified as the 'unknown woman' in the photograph?" Kelly never ceased to be amazed at just how self-involved he could be. Forget her; forget his wife; heck, even forget his kid; he was the real victim here.

"You're right. I'm sorry. I know your life is on the line also. We have to stick together and remain calm, so that we can decide what our next course of action needs to be. We can't lose our heads, or we'll start making mistakes. We have to determine if this is an old score, or if there is a new player. Either way, for all of our sakes, I have got to put an end to this."

"I will do whatever you ask, but I need to know that I can count on you, too." Kelly slowly crossed the distance between Christopher and her chair and began to massage his shoulders. "I mean, I know that your duties to the country will always come first for you. That's part of what makes you so special, but I also need to know that I'm important to you as well. I have to know that you won't just sacrifice me on the altar of your political ambitions."

"You know how I feel about you, but my constituents would crucify me if I abandoned my wife and child for my girlfriend, no matter how gorgeous she is." Christopher took Kelly's hand.

"I never said I wanted you to leave Tracy. Be real. The scandal alone would be enough to destroy both of our reputations. I said I was in love, not suicidal." Kelly smiled. In truth, she would never want to trade places with Tracy.

Christopher wasn't sure who had given the pictures to Tracy or who had leaked the photo to the press, but because it appeared that the media had not been given any of the more incriminating shots, he had to believe that the mystery leak wanted something more than just to embarrass his administration. He would just have to wait until he or she was ready to make the next move and hope that he could ward off further damage.

"You know that you're my priority. I sold my soul to you a long time ago," Christopher said. "We'll be okay if we stick together. What I need you to do is focus. I need you working on that speech. I go in front of the cameras in less than two hours, and I need to be brilliant." Christopher drew her close to him.

"Have I ever let you down?" Kelly smiled as she kissed his cheek.

****

"Good morning." Jennifer smiled through sleepy eyes as she stretched and ran her fingers through her hair. "I didn't hear you come home last night."

"I didn't want to wake you. I'm so sorry about last night. Time just got away from me."

"Don't worry about it. We'll survive. The dinner was for you anyway. You've been so stressed." She kissed his cheek. "What time are you and Justin leaving?"

Aaron looked bewildered.

"You are still taking him to regionals, right?"

"Oh, no, is that this weekend?"

Her face turned cold and angry. "Don't do this."

"I wish I didn't have to do this, but I have no choice. I only have three weeks left before I have to testify. I need every possible second I can get to prepare."

"You're telling him this time."

"Why don't you take him?"

"Because you're his father, and I didn't promise him."

"There will be other competitions. I would love to take him, but it's just impossible right now. I know he'll be disappointed, but it can't be helped. I need my family's support right now."

"He's been planning this since last month, which is before you were ever asked to testify before Congress."

"What should I do? I'm so swamped, and I haven't got a clue about how I'm going to catch up. There are tons of details to be finalized before the church's anniversary, and thanks to Mrs. Maple, I didn't finish my sermon for tomorrow. I have more things to do than time to do them."

"Then maybe you shouldn't have taken on anything new." She made no attempt to temper her tone as she usually did. This time she'd had it, and she wanted him to know it.

"What should I have done? Should I have turned them down? This is a critical time for the movement. This is important."

"So is being Justin's father."

"What is that supposed to mean?" Aaron went on the defensive. "Who do you think I'm doing this for?"

"Right. You 're doing all this for Justin." She could feel herself becoming increasingly angry with each passing moment.

"So what are you saying? Are you saying that I'm not there for my son?"

"I'm saying that you actually have to be here, in order to 'be there' for your son. Children don't raise themselves. I'm saying that I'm tired of being a single parent."

"I can't do this right now." Aaron grabbed his coat.

"Where are you going?" she demanded.

"Church."

"Whatever."

"We'll finish this later."

"I said whatever."

****

Victor stared at his wife as she sat across the table from him, eating her lunch. She was unusually quiet. He wondered if she suspected anything.

"I was surprised to see you. We never get together in the middle of the week just to have lunch anymore." Stacy smiled at her husband. "I thought for sure you would want to be there to support President Michaels in his hour of disgrace."

Victor searched his wife's face for any sign that she suspected his own indiscretion. He did not know what he would do in Christopher's position, but he did not intend to find out.

"How is he managing all this?" Stacy inquired. "I imagine it must be quite difficult. I'm sure the media hasn't given him a moment's peace.

"I haven't had an opportunity to speak to him, but I heard that Tracy left him." Realizing how strange it was for him not to have at least spoken to Christopher since the story broke, he made a mental note to call him as soon as he finished lunch. The last thing he needed at this point was to draw the suspicions of the White House. "I wanted to give him the opportunity to design the spin he wants to present, but I plan to call him."

"This has to be very hard on Tracy as well. Not everyone is strong enough to be married to a political giant."

"I can't even imagine how hard it must be to be the wife of a political figure. I'm really lucky to have you. I just wanted to make sure you know how much I love you. I don't think I spend enough time telling you how important you are to me."

"It has its perks."

"Thank you."

"For what?"

"Thank you for being my wife. Thank you for supporting me though everything. Having you by my side has allowed me to become the man I am," he proclaimed.

Stacy knew Victor better than he realized. This lunch was less about his love for her than his desire to reaffirm her love for him. Her usually inattentive husband was running scared. He was afraid that his extracurricular relationships were going to be exposed and that she might leave him. She smiled. She had always known about his many indiscretions, but as she had said, being the wife of a political figure had its perks. He was fortunate to have found a wife who understood the big picture.

"Of course I support you. I'll always support you. I'm your wife."

"I don't deserve you." Victor smiled. Now confidant that Stacy didn't suspect a thing, he returned to his meal.

Yes, but I deserve you, Stacy thought as she sipped her wine.

****

"I'll take a few more questions." Christopher pointed to a young female reporter just off center.

"Isn't morality your only real issue? It's no secret that your administration is overwhelmingly Christian. You yourself have rarely shied away from an opportunity to spout your 'life begins at conception' rhetoric. Isn't this just a thinly veiled attempt to legislate your own brand of morality?"

"I'm concerned about the potential for human rights abuses that surround this issue."

"Mr. President, are we to understand that you see no room for compromise?"

"Though I am at this time opposed to the lifting of the restrictions on the use of stem cells for research, and I support the current prohibition on human cloning, I don't exclude the possibility of revisiting this issue at a later time when there are more answers. As for right now, however, there are just too many ethical questions left unanswered, and I have a duty to the American people to demand that those issues be fully addressed before moving forward."

"What about your constituents who don't have that kind of time?" the young reporter pressed.

"I don't take this decision lightly. I know that someone will be negatively affected, no matter what I decide. That was my final question. Thank you."

"Mr. President, just one more question," a lone voice called out from the pressing crowd of reporters. "In light of pictures that have recently surfaced of you and an unidentified young woman, do you feel the need to reevaluate your stand on morality?"

"People will undoubtedly make their own assumption about what the pictures prove or don't prove, but as for my stand on morality, it is unchanged. What's right is right, and what's wrong is wrong. Morality has to be the compass we use to guide our actions, not the other way around."

"According to my sources, you and Mrs. Michaels have separated. Would you like to make a statement?"

There was silence.

"Excuse me, but this conferences was called to address the issues directly concerning human cloning and stem cells research," insisted Gregg Scott. He had only headed public relations for a year, and this was his first real opportunity to prove his value. He could not afford to let things get out of control.

"No, I'll address that," Christopher offered. "The allegations of an indiscretion have caused great pain to the people who love and trust me the most. My marriage is strong, and I am confident that we will survive this crisis. My wife and I, however, decided that it would be best for her to take our daughter away for a few weeks to protect her from all the negative publicity. I will be joining them as soon as possible. Out of respect for my family, I must decline making any further comments concerning my marriage. Thank you all."

Kelly watched from the wings as Christopher tried to explain away their affair. Her phone rang. She paused to hear the end of Christopher's speech. She smiled. He may have ad-libbed the final question without her help, but he was really great on his feet. She was impressed.

Christopher ended the conference. He hoped that his personal issues would not dwarf the real issues concerning cloning and stem-cell research, but deep down inside, he feared that may have been someone's intentions all along. As he left the podium, an aide handed him a slip of paper. It was from

Balile, requesting another meeting. Christopher folded the paper and placed it in his pocket.

Kelly felt the cell phone in her pocket vibrate. "Kelly here." Her expression became serious when she heard the voice on the other line. "He's just finishing. Everything is going as planned."

"That's good to hear. I have to hurry. I have an important meeting with the director to update the Triad on our progress. I'm delighted that I will be able to report such good news. I'll keep in touch." Balile smiled as he hung up the phone. He had been worried about how things would play out. He knew that he'd laid the proper foundation and had played all the right cards, but he also recognized that no one could fully predict the unpredictability of another. He picked up the phone to make one last call. "How is our girl holding up?" he asked.

"She's doing as well as can be expected. She is one of the strongest women I know," Sarah whispered.

"Great. She'll need every bit of that strength in the days to come. Stay close to her. We can't afford any mistakes at this point."

"I understand completely." She quickly put away her cell phone when she heard Katelyn returning from the kitchen.

"Who was that?"

"No one of any consequence. How is Talen?"

"He has his good and bad days, but lately there seem to be more bad days than good."

"I have really missed him."

"I know; he misses you, too. You're his only auntie. He loves hanging out with you. He used to really enjoy your standing monthly park date. He still talks about his last trip to the big city."

"I remember. That was the night he had that nasty fall. I felt horrible. How many stitches did he need?"

"Ten." Katelyn smiled as she remembered less complicated times. "You sounded like you had been crying. I couldn't tell who felt worse, you or Talen."

Sarah forced an uneasy smile. She had been crying. She cared about Talen more than her own grandkids, and delivering him into the hands of the Triad doctor to implant the device that would make him sick was the most difficult thing she had ever been called upon to do. Even now, the thought of that night still made her tremble. She spilled her tea. "I'm so sorry." She blinked away a tear.

Katelyn didn't notice as she rushed to get something to clean up the mess.

Sarah knew that Talen's death would not be in vain, but it did not make it any easier to watch someone she cared for die. She had been there when he was born. She had introduced his parents, so in a way, she felt like the instrument of both his creation and his demise.

****

It was late when Aaron returned home. He had spent the afternoon at the church, working on his speech. As he drove up to the house, he was surprised to see that Jennifer's car was gone. He had expected her home hours ago. He checked the messages as soon as he went in the house, but there were none from Jennifer. He tried to reach her on her cell phone, but she had obviously turned it off. Aaron started to worry. He knew that she had been upset, but it was not like her to stay out so late without leaving a message.

Aaron became more concerned with each passing moment. Concern was soon replaced by desperation. Aaron knew that Jennifer was right. He had been neglecting his duties as a father and as a husband. He hoped that he would get the opportunity to apologize to both her and Justin, and at least try to make things right.

As Aaron passed the den, he saw Justin's trophies from past competitions. There was a new one. He picked up the trophy and read the inscription. It was from earlier that day. Justin had won first place in his division. He smiled to himself as he returned the trophy to the shelf. He felt both proud and ashamed as he glanced at all the trophies Justin had won over the last two years. He had missed them all. Jennifer was right, he was missing an important part of their son's life, and if he didn't get his priorities straight, he was going to lose something very important: his relationship with his son. He had been spreading himself far too thin and spending way too much time away from his family. As a result, everything and everyone in his life was suffering.

The phone rang. He grabbed it before it could ring again. "Where are you?" He was relieved to hear her voice.

"About two hours from New Jersey. I decided to take a trip back to New York."

"When will you be home?"

"I'm not sure."

"What about Justin. He has school."

"He's doing well in school, and he hasn't missed many days. It will be easy for him to make up any work that he misses."

"I'm sorry about today."

"This isn't just about today. I wish it were."

"I've been under so much pressure," Aaron started to explain.

"And I haven't?"

"I know that you have."

"I can't keep doing this alone."

"I know, and things are going to get better. I'm going to make some changes," he promised.

"You've promised that before, but things have only gone from bad to worse."

"We need to talk," Aaron told her.

"I agree, but I need a few days alone to decide what's best for my son and for me."

"I understand. We'll talk when you get home."

"Count on it."

****

Christopher lay alone in bed, waiting for Tracy's call, as he imagined she must have done so many nights waiting for him. Her absence made the room feel overwhelmingly large and empty. He had often imagined what it would feel like to be single again, but he could not have imagined this. He missed her more than he ever thought possible.

She had agreed to call once she reached her destination. He looked at the clock; it was getting late. He knew that they had arrived safely, but she had not yet called. He had agreed to give her all the space she needed, but this was harder than he thought. Knowing that she might not ever return made her absence all the more unbearable. He needed his family back.

Christopher picked up the phone to call Tracy but forced himself to hang up. He might not be able to undo all the mistakes he'd made, but he could keep his promise to respect her need for space.

Christopher rolled over in the bed, stopping just short of Tracy's side. He gently caressed the pillow where Tracy had once rested her head. Why had it taken losing her for him to realize just how much she meant to him?

Christopher was asleep by the time Tracy's call was finally patched through to his room. It startled him.

"Hi, Christopher. Did I wake you?"

"No, I was just lying here thinking of you."

"How are things?" Tracy smiled. She'd been up all night thinking of him as well.

"They've been better. The big vote is in a few weeks, and things are looking pretty grim, not to mention that the press has been relentless."

"What are you going to do?"

"Stand my ground. Aaron is going to testify."

"He's such a great speaker. That has to help."

"I hope so, but the tide is not in my favor. Let's not spend our time talking about work."

"Then what?" she asked.

"I really miss you guys."

"We miss you, too. Loving you is not the problem."

"I know. I don't mean to pressure you."

"It's okay, but it is rather late. I'll remember you in my prayers."

"Will you call tomorrow?"

"Of course," she promised.

"Great. Hearing your voice makes things seem a little less hopeless."

"I know how hard this is for you, but I know we need this time to figure out if we are both willing to do what it will take to put this marriage back together."

"I'm willing to do whatever you say. Just tell me what you want me to do."

"It's not that simple. First, we need to understand how and why this happened. I don't want you to do what's right so that I'll come back to you. I want you to be faithful because you can't imagine doing anything else." Tracy wanted so much to give in to her husband and run back to him, but she knew that that would not fix their marriage. It would just be a temporary fix until the next time he felt attracted to another woman. "Good night."

"Until tomorrow, then?"

"Until tomorrow."

Christopher couldn't sleep. He could not wait until tomorrow.

****

When Jennifer had called her friend Trish Campbell to ask if she and Justin could stay for a few days, Trish had not hesitated. In fact, she was happy to welcome her friend, not to mention that she was more than slightly anxious to learn what had driven Jennifer back to New York in the middle of the night without warning—and without Aaron.

It had been far too long since their last visit. Even though Trish was older, as a fellow pastor's wife, there were things only she could understand. Trish eagerly escorted Jennifer to the guest room, as Pastor Campbell carried a sleeping Justin into the house and laid him in their daughter's old room before he unloaded Jennifer's car.

Jennifer and Trish made small talk as she unpacked. They talked about everything from the church's impending anniversary to the weather but not about what was truly bothering her. As much as Jennifer needed to talk to

Trish, she felt that doing so might be betraying Aaron, so she continued to talk about everything else.

"It sounds like Justin is awake. I should have warned Pastor Campbell that Justin isn't the same quiet child he remembers," Jennifer joked. "I hope Justin doesn't wear him out."

"I'm sure he's enjoying the stimulating conversation," Trish laughed. "Besides, it's good for a pastor to be on the receiving end from time to time.

"Tell me about it."

"Why don't you?"

"What?" Jennifer asked.

"Why don't you tell me the real reason you're here."

Jennifer stopped unpacking and sat on the side of the bed. "Am I that obvious?"

"Only to those who know and love you," Trish whispered, "and I've been a pastor's wife for more than a few years. Not much gets past me. So tell me … where is Aaron?"

"He's home." Jennifer broke down and told her friend what was bothering her. Trish listened as Jennifer unloaded her problems. As the wife of a pastor, she'd become quite a good listener, and at that moment, that was exactly what Jennifer needed most.

"We had an argument," Jennifer explained.

"That must have been some argument if it drove you all the way up here. Is there someone else?"

"No! It's nothing like that."

"Then tell me. There isn't much I haven't heard before."

Jennifer brushed away the tears stinging her eyes. "He's too busy for us. He's either preaching or teaching all the time. He's never home anymore. I know that it sounds like I'm jealous of God, but I miss my husband. I know that sounds silly."

"Honey, there's nothing wrong with you, and God knows that you're not jealous. Being a pastor is being on call for God, 24/7. It just takes time to learn to balance the responsibilities of being a pastor and a family man. Have faith in your relationship. Do you still love him?"

"I could never stop loving him. I'm just not sure I can continue to live with him."

Trish listened as Jennifer recounted the struggles she and Aaron were experiencing. Trish did not judge, nor did she take sides. She didn't even offer her friend advice. She understood how important it was for Jennifer to seek God and figure things out on her own.

"I've been alone for a long time now. He's gone more than he's home, and that's not fair to Justin or to me." Jennifer sighed. "You're not going to tell me what to do are you?"

"Is that what you came for?"

"I guess not."

"Besides, you know me better than that. I can only advise you based on my limited knowledge of the situation, so however well-meaning it would be, any advice I give you would be flawed. Only God knows everything, including what you should do. It's not a secret that he's keeping from you. If you ask him, he'll tell you exactly what you should do."

"Was I wrong to leave?"

"No. Sometimes a husband needs a kick in the pants to make the necessary changes. This may be just the wake-up call Aaron needs."

"How do you know so much?"

"Let's just say Pastor Campbell hasn't always been so good at balancing his duties." Trish smiled and handed her friend a tissue.

Jennifer sighed. Trish was right, as usual. She knew that Trish would point her in the right direction; that was why she had come. "I know I have to seek God for myself," Jennifer said.

"Yes, you do, but you have a safe place here while you are doing that."

"Thanks."

The two women sat talking for hours.

****

Angela awoke in the middle of the night and reached for her husband in the dark. He was not there. She got out of the bed to look for Neal and found him sitting on the porch, staring into space.

"Are you all right?" She gently caressed his arm.

"I'm fine. You should go back to bed," Neal reassured her.

"I know you better than that. You're worried about seeing your brother. You're afraid he's going to hate you."

"Why shouldn't he?"

"He can't hate you. You're his brother."

"That's right. I'm the brother who abandoned him, just when he needed me most."

"You did what you had to do. You weren't given a choice. Everything you did, you did for him. It was just as hard on you as it was on him. It's was even worse for you, because he had Sarah. Who did you have?"

"I hope he sees it that way, but somehow I doubt it."

"Then we'll have to help him see. Everything depends upon it."

He softly kissed her lips. "I'm lucky to have you."

"Yeah, and don't you forget it."

"If I do, I'm sure you'll remind me."

"You better believe it." Angela took Neal by the hand and led him to their bedroom.

Chapter Seventeen

Eric's plane was late arriving. Sharay waited patiently. He wasn't expecting her, but she hoped that he wouldn't be annoyed. His visits home often left him emotionally drained, so he liked to be left alone a day or two after his return. She looked up from her magazine just in time to see him approaching.

"What are you doing here?"

"I came to pick you up," Sharay explained.

"I have my car."

"I know, but we need to talk. I'll bring you back to get your car."

"Did something happen?"

"I'll explain everything, but you have to trust me," she said as they made their way through the terminal.

"This sounds serious."

"It is. I wouldn't be here otherwise. Do you have any checked bags?"

"No. I just have the one carry-on." He held up the DNA collection kit she'd given him. "There's no need to carry a suitcase, since I have clothes at home."

Sharay led him to her car.

As she pulled into the hotel driveway, Eric vehemently protested. He wasn't in the mood for games. The only bed he wanted to see was the one in his apartment.

"It's not what you think. We're meeting someone here."

Eric followed her into the hotel. He could tell that she was worried. She reluctantly knocked on the door.

"What's wrong?" he asked. "Who are we here to meet?"

"I want you to try to keep an open mind. Hear him out before you decide how you feel about things."

The door opened. Instinctively, Eric took a step back. At first, he imagined that his eyes were deceiving him—he couldn't believe what he was seeing. He grabbed the doorframe to steady himself. He opened his mouth, but the only sound to escape his trembling lips was the sound of him gasping for air. It felt as if he'd lost the ability to breathe as well as the power to speak.

"It's all right, Eric. We can explain," Sharay assured him.

"You're …" He gasped for air. "You're dead. I identified your body. I was at your funeral."

"It wasn't me."

"What are saying?"

"Come inside and I'll explain."

****

When Balile arrived at the home of the director, he was met by the director's twelve-year-old daughter, Lidia. She was quite lovely. Balile figured she had to take after her mother, as she looked nothing like her father. The young girl escorted him to the den, where he waited for his host.

"I hope you haven't been waiting long."

"No, I just arrived. Your lovely daughter was a perfect hostess."

"Yes, she serves her purpose. She makes my wife happy and keeps her out of my hair."

Balile chuckled, believing that the director was joking, but stopped abruptly when it became apparent that he was not.

"My wife should get all the credit—she did select Lidia."

Balile realized that Lidia must have been chosen from among the abducted children. He listened intently as the director carefully explained the Triad's plans and their expectations for him and his team.

"What about the boy? I've been alerted that he does not look well, and that the toll this illness is placing on his young body may have permanent, if not fatal, consequences."

"You've been involved long enough to figure out where this is all heading. The impending birth is where your focus needs to be. Once the promised one has arrived, we will no longer need this child."

Balile was not shocked by the director's comment. He had begun to suspect as much.

"The Triad agrees," the director continued. "After we are sure that Sharay has been successful, we will take care of it. No one will know. He will just succumb to his illness and pass quietly away in his sleep."

"Isn't there another way?" Balile wasn't sure how Neal was going to take the news. Though he had not met the boy, Talen was still his brother's child.

"No. There can be only one. Talen is not important; it was never about him. He was only a means to an end."

****

Eric sat across from his brother. He had never expected to see him again, and he couldn't stop staring. Sharay sat beside him and tried to take his hand. He snatched his hand away.

"Were you part of this charade?" he demanded.

"No!"

"Don't blame Sharay. She didn't know anything. We only met a couple of days ago. I contacted her because I needed her help to reach you. She wanted to call you right away, but I asked her to let me talk to you first. I know that you have questions."

Eric didn't know what to say. It was true. He had so many questions, but he wasn't sure he wanted to know the answers. He couldn't imagine what excuse his brother could possibly give that would explain what he'd done? What excuse would be good enough to explain this level of betrayal and justify all that he'd suffered?

"Say something," Neal said. "Tell me what you are thinking. I can imagine how my death must have affected you."

Eric shook his head violently. "No, you have no idea. You can't have any idea, or there is no way you would think anything you have to say could possibly make one bit of difference. You were all I had left! When you died, I had nothing. I had no one. I was all alone."

"I'm so sorry." Neal heard the pain in his brother's voice. He wanted to say the right thing to make things right between them, but nothing seemed enough. It had all seemed to make sense all those years ago. The Triad had determined that Neal's "death" would put an end to any chance of Eric's finding God and would renew Eric's commitment to the cause. When Neal had been ordered to fake his own death to help get Eric back on track, he'd thought it was only going to be for a short while. He never expected so many years to pass before seeing his brother face to face again.

"Did you know that I blamed myself?" Eric moaned. He felt so conflicted. While he wanted so much to hate Neal, he needed to hug him even more. "I felt like your death was my fault. After all, you joined the Marines so that you could provide for me and send me to college. I was the reason you put yourself in harm's way. How did you think I was going to feel about your death—or did you think about me at all?"

"My whole life was about taking care of you. It *is* about taking care of you."

"How was your leaving taking care of me? Were you tired? Did you just need a break? Help me understand."

"Do you remember when our parents died?" Neal asked gently.

"What do our parents have to do with you faking your own death and leaving me to grieve for you? I still visit your grave every year."

"Everything. Do you remember how they died?"

"They were in a car accident."

"What else?" Neal encouraged him. "Tell me the specifics."

Eric sighed. "Dad was driving and Mom was injured. He couldn't get over his feelings of guilt, so he focused his feelings elsewhere. He became paranoid. He kept talking about someone poisoning her and how he should have listened to her. A few weeks later, he went into a state of depression and shot himself in a motel room with me asleep in the next room. An officer called you, and you came to get me."

"That's only half right?"

"What's that suppose to mean?"

"Do you remember how Mom would disappear—for days, sometimes?"

"I remember. Dad use to say that she wasn't well."

"She was sick, but her illness was in her head. She was being tormented by her fear that your life was in danger and that only God could save you. Dad tried to get help for her, but then she got mixed up with some religious fanatics who believed her story. She trusted them more than her own family. She planned to hand you over to them. I don't know what they would have done to you, but Dad wasn't going to find out. He wouldn't let her give you to them. He ordered her to stay away from them."

"So Mom was crazy; yeah, I get it. What does that have to do with anything? What does that have to do with what you did?"

"You don't get it."

"Then help me understand. I really need to understand."

Neal took a deep breath and forced himself to continue. "Dad didn't take you to that motel to kill himself."

"What are saying? Of course he did. Don't forget; I was there."

"So was I."

Eric was shocked. He didn't know what Neal meant, but he knew that he'd been alone with his father when they went to the motel that night.

"And Mom didn't just die. She was poisoned."

Eric's eyes narrowed. His mind was reeling. "Poisoned by whom?"

"Who knows? I always suspected those freaks that she called her friends, but Dad blamed himself—and you. He was convinced that there was a conspiracy that involved you. Our mother and her friends believed that you were on a destructive path and that your destiny had to be altered. Our father believed that she had been poisoned by people trying to protect you. He took you to that motel to meet her friends. He was going to honor her final wishes and give you to them."

"That's a lie!" Eric protested. It had to be a lie, or everything he'd believed his whole life was a lie. He stood to leave.

Neal stopped him. "I wish it were. I got there just in time. He hadn't had a chance to make the final arrangements. I tried to convince him to give you to me, but he refused. He kept talking crazy."

Eric felt a cold chill as he began to reevaluate his entire childhood. He reflected on how his mother's insanity and involvement with religious fanatics had led to her death, and how as a result, his own father had wanted him dead. He tried to accept that the person he trusted most, his brother, had had a good reason to fake his own death and abandon him. Everything Eric had believed about his life had been a lie, and he wasn't sure if he wanted to hear any more.

Neal could not bring himself to say the rest. He reached for his brother, but Eric pulled away. There were some things that Neal had hoped to take with him to his grave. This was one: "Our father admitted that he had drugged you. I tried to get you out, but …"

"What did you do?"

Neal looked away. He'd already gone too far to stop. He knew that he had to tell him the rest.

Eric's mouth dropped open as he came to a sudden realization. "You killed him, didn't you?"

"I saved you. He wouldn't let me take you. He had a gun. We struggled, and the gun went off. I swear that it was an accident."

"Why didn't you just tell the police what happened?"

"I couldn't. I knew that I'd be cleared eventually, but who knew how long that would take. Both of our parents were dead, and we had no other family. You would have been alone, and I couldn't let that happen. You needed me. That was all that mattered. I cleaned up the room and planted the gun in Dad's hand to make it look like a suicide. Dad had drugged you, so I knew you wouldn't wake up and find him. I called the authorities and reported hearing a gunshot, and then I just waited for them to call."

Eric sat silently as he listened to the rest of what Neal had to say. Neal explained that once he learned that Eric was involved with the same religious sect that—either directly or indirectly—had caused their mother's death, he was compelled to act. He explained that he had been afraid that they would find Eric and that his life, once again, would be in danger.

Neal wanted to tell Eric everything, but Balile was right. He stopped just short of explaining the Triad's concerns about Eric's newfound religion. Instead, he led Eric to believe that he feared for his physical safety and that he had drawn the fanatics' attention away from his brother and faked his own death to permanently throw them off Eric's trail.

"Why didn't you tell me?" Eric asked. "I could have helped you. We could have fought them together."

"It was the only way I knew to protect you."

"Why didn't you ever try to contact me later?"

"What would you have done?"

"I would have joined you."

"Exactly. As I said, I couldn't risk your life." Neal needed Eric to understand. "I was willing to pay any price for your happiness."

"What about your happiness?"

"I can't complain. I met my wife, Angela, while I was checking into Sharay's past. I had to make sure my baby brother wasn't going to get hooked up with the wrong girl. Angela and I hit it off right away and decided to get married a few months later."

Eric eyed Angela uncomfortably, as he remembered their night together.

"I know what you're thinking, and I know all about it." Neal winked at Angela. "Angela and I don't have any secrets. We have an open relationship, so you see, everything worked out for the best."

"Do you call this 'working out'?"

"Yes, I do. You're angry right now, but at least you're alive to be angry with me. If anything had happened to you, then everything I did to protect you would have been for nothing. Please don't get me wrong; I don't regret any of it, but I need for it to have meant something."

"Then what has changed?" Eric needed to know.

"I'm here to help."

"What can you do? Are you going to help me find a cure?"

"That's exactly why he's here," Sharay interjected.

"I don't understand."

"I know some very powerful people who are eager to help," Neal explained.

"Why?"

"Does it matter?"

"Yes. After all these years, I'd say that it matters."

****

"Hello, Aaron."

"Hey, Christopher, how are things going?"

"Forget about me; how are you?"

"I guess you've heard. Bad news sure travels quickly. How did you hear?"

"My mom called earlier."

"Your mom? Oh, yeah, I guess Jennifer must be staying with the Campbells. I'm sure the whole church must know by now." Aaron shook his head. He had hoped to keep their personal problems private.

"Jennifer is being discreet, but people do talk. They want to know where you are. They're concerned."

"I'm sure they are."

"Why didn't you call me?" Christopher asked. "I always call you when I screw up."

"There wasn't anything you could do, and you have your own problems right now."

"I've always got crap going on in my life. Such is the life of a screw-up. You've always been there for me. Let me help you right now. It's my chance to be the giver for once. Heck, I'd just appreciate working on someone else's problems for a change."

"You know, to make matters worse, I know she's completely right. I can't blame her. She should have left me. I left her emotionally long before she left me. I've been a bad husband and father."

"I don't believe that. You've just been distracted. You have so much on your plate. You can fix this," Christopher encouraged him.

"I wish I could be sure of that. As horribly as I've disappointed them, they gave me another chance, and I failed them miserably. I just hope you're right."

"What can I do to help?"

"Nothing. I'm going to have to give her some time to decide what she wants to do. The ball is completely in her court this time."

"You should call her," Christopher suggested.

"I have, but she's not ready to talk to me. She's heard it all before. I don't think there is anything I can say to convince her that I've learned my lesson, and that things will be different this time."

"What do you think she's going to do?"

"I'm not sure," Aaron admitted. "I hope she'll come home, but if not, I'll go to her."

"What if she stays in New York?"

"I'll move back to New York. If necessary, I'll spend the rest of my life trying to fix what I broke," Aaron insisted.

"Do you really mean that?"

"Of course."

"Then tell her that," Christopher advised his friend. "If you really mean what you are saying, then don't wait for her to make up her mind to leave you. Tell her now, while it doesn't seem like a final desperate ploy to manipulate her into forgiving you."

"Thanks."

"At least someone should learn from my mistakes," Christopher said sadly.

"What about you? Have you heard from Tracy?"

"She says she needs more time. She says she needs a few more days, weeks, or maybe months to decide what to do with the rest of her life. She's not sure she wants me in it yet, but she is sure she's not ready to rush back into a marriage that she feels is 'devoid of respect.'"

"She said that?"

"Yeah, and she's right. Somewhere down the line, I forgot my vows. She's never going to forgive me. I don't expect her to."

"Did she say that?"

"No, but …" Christopher sighed heavily.

"No 'but,'" Aaron cautioned him. "What are you willing to give up to save your own marriage?"

"Everything," Christopher admitted.

"Then take your own advice. Tell her that."

"I don't think it will be enough. You're guilty of being a jerk; I'm guilty of being a cheat."

"I cheated. I cheated every time I went to the church when I should have gone home. I cheated every time I accepted a speaking engagement when I already had plans with my family. I cheated every time I took on a new responsibility without knowing how I was going to handle the ones I already had."

"So we are both cheaters."

"I guess we both have a lot of work to do. We have to get or priorities in order, and do it fast before we lose everything that is important to us."

Aaron hung up the phone. He felt overwhelmed by feelings of loss. He'd done exactly what Pastor Campbell had warned him against. He'd lost sight of the people who were most important to him. He picked up the phone to call Jennifer.

Chapter Eighteen

Sharay checked the viability of her samples.

"What's the news?" Eric asked hesitantly.

She smiled. "Well, Eric, I would like to introduce you to your son."

Eric could not believe it. He grabbed Sharay and kissed her. He had never loved her as much as he did at that moment. She had given him back his future. No matter what happened or didn't happen, he knew that some part of his son would live on.

"What do we do now?"

"Now you invite me home." She winked at him.

"That's not funny."

"It's not meant to be. I want you to introduce me to your wife as a specialist. I'm going to examine your wife to 'take samples' to use in our research. I'll implant the embryo then."

"What do I need to do?" he asked.

"Sleep with your wife." Sharay was suddenly serious. The thought of him and Katelyn together sickened her, but there was no other way.

****

As Marcus sat across the table from Kira, he found his mind wandering to his last meeting with Neal—the meetings always left him feeling anxious.

"I'm so happy you called. I really wish I got into the city more often." Kira smiled. Despite their age difference, she was attracted by his dark eyes, long lashes, and full lips.

"So do I. So what does bring you here, not that I'm at all complaining," he flirted. "My parents didn't mention that you would be speaking at the next meeting."

"That's not why I'm here."

"What's bothering you? I can tell that you have something on your mind." Marcus shifted uncomfortably in his chair. Did she suspect him? Had she told anyone?

"I had a dream."

Marcus laughed but stopped abruptly when he realized that she was serious.

"I had a dream that we were all in danger. I dreamed of a snake in the Garden of Eden. Everyone saw the snake, but it was small and insignificant, so everyone ignored it. No one did anything. Then the small, insignificant snake gave birth to an entire clutch of larger more deadly snakes, one of which was the most dangerous viper of them all … but by then it was too late."

"I'm confused. Are you saying that you came home because of a nightmare?"

"I came home to talk to my mother about my dream."

"Now I understand. She's going to interpret your dream, right?"

"I don't need her to interpret such an obvious dream. It means that we are under attack from within," she explained.

"If you don't need her help to interpret the dream, then what do you need her to do?"

"My mother use to have dreams like mine," Kira explained. "She said it was like knowing that she was at the threshold of a great war and not being able to stop it."

"I don't understand."

"I know." She smiled and gently touched his hand.

****

Eric picked up the phone to call Katelyn to tell her about their progress but then decided against it. He wished he could share his excitement with her, but he knew that that would be impossible. She could never know what he'd done. She would never understand. He knew that she would view it as a betrayal. She would see it as a confirmation that he had given up on saving their son, instead of its being a final attempt to preserve some small part of him, if all else failed.

"What's up, little brother?" Neal asked. "You looked a million miles away. Is something wrong?"

"No. Actually, I just received some amazing news."

"Well, don't leave me hanging. Tell me this amazing news."

"Sharay was successful. She'll be ready for implantation in a few short weeks."

"That's wonderful news." Neal was excited to learn of Sharay's success. He was certain that the Triad would be just as pleased. Everything was going as planned. They could not have hoped for anything more, but it did not escape him that Eric was obviously not as excited as he would have expected. "But why aren't you thrilled?"

"I am," Eric insisted.

"But …?"

"This is great news, but it doesn't change the facts. My son is still sick, and I am no closer to finding a cure.

"You're doing all you can."

"That's not enough."

"It will have to be." Neal knew that Talen's fate had been sealed. "What more can you ask of yourself? You have to stop worrying about things you don't control. Sometimes, all you can do is cut your losses."

"How can you say that to me?" Eric snapped. "He's my son, and I'll fight to save him with my last breath. I'll never give up on him—never."

"No, of course not, but the Triad is on top of this. You have to trust us. We have given you the best researchers to help you. At some point it's out of our hands, but until then, the Triad will do everything humanly possible to ensure your success."

"So you keep telling me. You know, that still confuses me."

"What?" Neal asked.

"You're right; they've done more for me than I've had a right to ask, so I'm wondering, why me? I'm a pretty good scientist, but I'm not so conceited as to think that I'm the best by any stretch of the imagination. So why me? Why do they care so much about me and my family?"

"Why does it matter? Haven't they done all they promised? They are completely funding your and Sharay's research."

"Nothing is free, and if there is going to be a price to be paid, I'd like to know what to expect." Eric wanted answers, and he wasn't letting it go this time.

Neal was annoyed by Eric's lack of trust, but he also understood that he hadn't been given much of a reason to have faith."

"You were chosen," Neal stated flatly.

"I was chosen? By whom and for what purpose?"

"You were selected by the Triad to be the father of our future and to help usher in a golden age, so to speak." Neal watched Eric's expression turn to one of annoyance. "I know that this may sound a little strange."

"Did you say a *little* strange? Please tell me you're kidding. You can't believe in all this hocus-pocus religious crap."

"I've seen enough to know that there is more in this world than what we can see and feel. Not everything has a simple explanation."

"You sound like one of those Christian fanatics," Eric berated him.

"I'm not a Christian. I don't serve an invisible god. I serve the Triad. We both do."

"I serve myself and my family."

"And in doing so, you serve the purpose of the Triad. You were chosen by the Triad for this purpose."

"Why me? Why was I chosen?" Eric asked.

"Actually, you chose yourself the day you were born."

"What's that suppose to mean?"

"You were born on our most holy day."

"June 6?"

"In 2006."

Eric collapsed into a chair, laughing hysterically. "I may not know a whole lot about this religion stuff, so correct me if I'm wrong, but isn't the number 666 supposed to be a sign of evil?"

"That is only true for those who don't understand."

"Let me guess—you understand, right?"

"I know more than you think."

"Fine. You've got my attention. Explain it to me."

"Many women within the Triad attempted to time the birth of their children with this holy day. Some women even had their labor induced, but there were only twenty-seven natural male births, and of those twenty-seven, you were selected," Neal explained.

"Our mother was a member of the Triad?"

"Both of our parents were."

"You mean the same Triad that heads the Center and has been funding my research?"

"Yes, and also arranged for Sarah to take us in after our parents' death, and provided your college scholarship, and got you the job at Grayson. You even owe your family to the Triad. Who do you think arranged for Sarah to introduce you and Katelyn?"

"You make it sound as though they have been orchestrating my entire life."

"In many ways, they have."

Eric listened as Neal explained how the Triad had been involved at every juncture in his life, from the time he was born. Eric's anger at being manipulated was quickly replaced by concern. He was worried about the well-being of his family. It was obvious that the Triad was an extremely powerful entity, if not dangerous, and he wasn't comfortable with the level of preoccupation they were showing his family.

"I'm not saying that I believe this, but if what you say is true, that only explains their interest in me. What does this have to do with my family?"

"Your wife was chosen as well."

"Why?"

"What do you really know about your wife? Do you know Katelyn's true identity or even her true birthday?" Neal asked.

"Of course I don't. No one does. Her parents died in a horrible car accident when she was very young. They were never able to determine the identity of her parents. Katelyn's real name and birthday are just a couple of the many secrets they took with them to their graves."

"That's not exactly true. There were those who knew exactly who your wife's parents were and what her birthday is."

Eric's patience was wearing thin. He couldn't imagine why any of this should make any difference. "If there were those who knew who my wife's parents were, then why didn't they come forward? Why would they allow her to be placed in foster care? It doesn't make sense."

"In order to come forward, they would have had to expose far too much. They did what they felt they had to do for the greater good."

"Are you saying that my wife's parents were also members of the Triad?"

"Her father is a member of the elite."

"You said 'is.'" Eric couldn't believe what he was hearing. "Is her father still alive?"

"Both of her parents are, but only her father knows where she is."

"What about her mother?" Eric pressed.

"Her mother has been forbidden to reveal herself to Katelyn." Neal hesitated. He had already said more than he had intended. "Sarah is Katelyn's mother."

Eric felt as if he had been punched in the gut.

"As much as you might want to tell her, you can't"

"What do you think you can possibly say that would stop me?"

"As I said, to tell her the truth you would have to expose far too much. Are you ready to tell her about your baby? How about telling her about Sharay? We've all gone too far. We have to play this thing to the end."

"Why would they do this?"

"Katelyn needed to be immersed into the Christian world. It will give your son a unique advantage against his enemies," Neal explained.

"He's a baby. What enemies could he possibly have?"

"We are not the only ones who believe in the prophesy. Have you heard of the FLOCK?"

"Of course I've heard of them. They are religious zealots, determined to thrust the entire planet back into the Middle Ages."

"I'm glad to hear that you feel that way."

"How else would I feel? They stand for superstition, intolerance, and ignorance—everything that I struggle against. They are the most vocal opponents to stem-cell research in the country, and their members have clout. They reach all the way to the White House. They practically single-handedly bankrolled the current administration's entire campaign."

"Yes, and they are the most dangerous opponents to the Triad's future plans."

"That doesn't explain what was done to my wife."

"When the time comes, your progeny will be able to walk freely between both camps."

"My 'progeny' is back at home, fighting for his life, and if I don't find a cure soon, he won't be walking anywhere."

"If you trust us and do as we say, together, we'll move mountains—one mountain in particular."

Eric still didn't trust the Triad's motives, and he wasn't sure he was ready to put the entire fate of his family in their hands, but if there was even a slight chance of saving his son, he would have sold his soul to the devil himself. "What do I need to do?"

Chapter Nineteen

"Hi, Tracy, I wasn't expecting to hear from you today." Christopher was delighted to hear her voice.

"I couldn't sleep."

"Is anything wrong?" He sat up in the bed.

"I want to come home."

"Nothing would make me happier! When?"

"No listen. I want to come home, but only if you're sure you're prepared to fully commit to this marriage."

"I am, and I promise I'll never give you reason to doubt my commitment again."

"That's good, because it won't be easy. Forgiveness is a gift, but trust has to be earned," she explained.

"I'm ready to do whatever it takes to win back your trust. I will never be unfaithful again. I don't even know why this happened in the first place. You are all I've ever wanted, and I love you so much. I didn't love her. In fact, I've never loved any woman but you."

"And you're the only man that I've ever loved as well, but I'm not finished. For starters, she has to go."

"I've already ended my relationship with her."

"I don't know who she is, and it's really not even important. It doesn't even matter if there have been others before her."

"No. She was—"

"Please let me finish." Tracy took a deep breath. "It doesn't matter, because that was the past, and you can't change that no matter how much you try. The past can only destroy us if we let it, but there is something very dangerous about this woman."

"I don't understand."

"I can't fully explain to you how I know this, but everything inside of me tells me that this woman is a real threat to us—not just to our marriage or your career but to our health as well. I believe she has an agenda that will destroy all of us if we don't stop her."

"I'm willing to do whatever it takes," Christopher promised. "I'll take care of it."

"I love you."

"I love you, too. I can't wait to see you."

Christopher checked the time. It was late. He knew that Kelly would probably already be in bed, but he also knew what had to be done. He picked up the phone.

****

Sharay had not expected to like Katelyn, but despite herself, she understood what had drawn Eric to her. She was as kind as she was beautiful. With all that she was going through with the illness of her child, she still managed to smile warmly as she welcomed Sharay into their home for the first time. Sharay almost hated lying to her, but she reminded herself that she was there to help them.

Sharay explained the tests she wanted to run and how she intended to use any samples she collected. She also explained why it had been so important to perform a pregnancy test to ensure that Katelyn was not already pregnant. Though she claimed that it was standard procedure to ensure the safety of any child Katelyn might unknowingly be carrying, the truth was that they needed to ensure that the impending pregnancy would be the result of the implantation and not through ordinary means. Until then, Eric had been instructed to avoid having sex with his wife.

Katelyn had consented to the test for Sharay's peace of mind; the test results confirmed what Katelyn already knew—that she was not pregnant. With the pregnancy test out of the way, Sharay arranged for them to meet at Katelyn's hospital, where, as a favor to Katelyn, the hospital had granted her laboratory space to perform her tests. The two women finished their coffee while Eric spent time with Talen.

To Eric's delight, Talen seemed to have regained much of his strength. He could have almost forgotten that Talen was sick. They took Talen's puppy, Journey, for a long walk to allow Katelyn and Sharay an opportunity to discuss what Katelyn could expect over the next several weeks, while Sharay ran her tests.

"I'm so happy to have you here," Katelyn said genuinely. "Eric has told me how invaluable you have been to him in his research. You can't imagine how grateful we are. Before you offered to help, we had begun to lose all hope. With the exception of Sarah and a handful of his co-workers from his old lab donating their free time, all of Eric friends in the science community abandoned us. Talen is our only child. He means the world to us, and you have given us reason to hope again."

"I'm happy to help. Eric is a great friend and … um. I'm just glad I could make a difference." Sharay forced an uncomfortable smile.

Katelyn pretended not to notice. If Sharay could help save her son, Katelyn was willing to pretend that she didn't know that the woman was sleeping with her husband.

"Can I offer you anything else to eat? I know that you must be starving after your trip," Katelyn offered.

"No, I really should be going to the hotel. I'm exhausted, and we have an early day tomorrow."

"Eric and Talen seem to still be enjoying their walk. Maybe I can give you a ride to the hotel."

"That won't be necessary. I rented a car. It's parked in front of your neighbor's house. I hope they won't mind."

"Oh, no, we have great neighbors. I actually attend a local church with a few of them."

"I didn't know that you were a Christian."

"Well, I only recently started attending church again, but I used to be quite an active member when I was younger. One of my foster families use to take all of us kids to church every Sunday, but I never made my own commitment until recently. One of my neighbors took me to her church, and I don't know. It just felt right. It felt like coming home."

"How nice for you." Sharay could not believe that a woman as intelligent as Katelyn could subscribe to such superstitions.

As if reading Sharay's thoughts, Katelyn tried to explain. "You want to know how I can worship in the face of such despair."

Sharay stood to leave. "It's none of my business. Maybe I just don't understand how you can worship a God that has abandoned you."

"God has not abandoned me. He gives me the courage and strength to face each new day. Belief is a leap of faith. It is that belief that gets me through the day. You see, I know that no matter what happens here in this world, my son will be healed, and we will be together."

"I hope that works out for you."

"I'm staking our salvation on it."

"I'll stick to science, if you don't mind."

Katelyn nodded. "To each his own."

Chapter Twenty

Katelyn was thrilled to call Eric. She excitedly shared her pregnancy test results with him. "It had to have happened right after Sharay ran those second pregnancy tests."

"I am so excited. This is the best news we've had in over a year. I can't wait until this weekend. We'll do something special to celebrate." He was so thrilled to hear the joy in Katelyn's voice that he didn't even have to fake his excitement.

"Who was that?" Sharay asked as she finished dressing.

"Katelyn. She just found out that she's pregnant." Eric pulled on his pants.

"What took her so long? You'd think a doctor would be more in touch with her own body."

"She has a lot on her plate right now."

"Don't we all?" Sharay left without saying good-bye.

****

Marcus sat in the small diner, waiting for Neal. He hated the diner, with its low ceiling and dingy walls that seemed to close in on him—it was claustrophobic. It reminded him of a coffin. He slowly sipped his coffee, hoping to make the time go by more quickly, but before he realized it, he was finishing his third cup.

"I hope you haven't been waiting long."

"No. It's fine. I've only been here about—"

"That was rhetorical."

"Sorry."

"Let's just get down to things. I've got a lot to do."

Neal liked the diner. He chose it for their meetings because it never had more than a couple of patrons at a time and the waitresses were too inattentive to interrupt them.

Neal placed a photo on the table. Marcus picked it up to get a better look. It was a photo of a woman and a young boy. There was an address written on the back.

Neal pointed to the young boy in the photo. "He's your target. I want you to bring him to me alive. I don't care about the others, as long as the boy is unharmed. Do you understand?"

"Yes, but isn't there already someone in place who handles acquisitions?" Marcus asked.

"This won't be an acquisition as much as it is an execution. There should be at least one casualty, preferably the mother. The Triad feels the more visual the better."

"When?"

"Within the next two days. The boy and his mother are unexpectedly in town, but we are not sure for how long they'll be here."

"I understand. I'll take care of it right way."

"I knew you would." Neal threw a twenty on the table as they left the diner. "Make sure there are no mistakes."

"There won't be." Marcus watched Neal drive away; then he headed to the subway.

All the way home, Marcus thought of the unsuspecting family whose lives it was his job to destroy. A year ago, he would have been able to do this without so much as a thought, but something inside of him had changed. Despite his best efforts, he cared about this young boy and his mother. The boy didn't look much older than he had been when the Triad destroyed his life. He hated knowing that he was about to do something even more horrible to this child.

****

Kelly awoke early that morning and prepared to go into the office early. She was surprised to receive Christopher's invitation. She put on his favorite outfit and sexiest underwear. She planned to remind him why he enjoyed her company to ensure her place in his life. He'd obviously been pulling away from her since Tracy had discovered his indiscretion. Kelly had become concerned that he might be planning to end their relationship in order to win back his wife.

Kelly put the finishing touches on Christopher's speech before heading to his office. She didn't expect to have time that night—she planned to be otherwise occupied. She smiled to herself and unfastened another button before she confidently made her way to Christopher's private offices. She wished they could meet in the Oval Office, but Christopher preferred using his private offices for personal meetings.

"I was surprised to hear from you. I was beginning to think you were avoiding me." Kelly began to unbutton her blouse.

Christopher stopped her. "I'm sorry. I should not have left you in the dark."

"It's okay. I forgive you." She brushed the hair out of her face. "I'm just glad that you've decided to let me back into your life."

"Actually, that is why I've asked you to join me."

"Yes, I know."

"I love my wife, and if I'm going to have any chance at saving my marriage, I'm going to have to end things with you."

"I'm sorry—I'm a little confused. You asked me here so that you could … break up with me?"

"I didn't want to do it over the phone," he explained. "I felt I owed you that much."

"You owe me a lot more than that."

"That may be, but that is all I can offer."

"You don't have to do this. She doesn't even suspect it's me. You can say it was someone else and tell her that you've ended things." Kelly pouted. "She's a woman, and she loves you. She'll believe you because she needs to believe you."

"You're not listening."

"Yes, I am. You want Tracy to take you back!"

"No. I want my marriage back. As long as you're in the middle, there can never be true intimacy between Tracy and me. You and I cannot continue to share things that I should only be sharing with my wife."

"What about me?" she asked.

"I'm not abandoning you. I've arranged for you to get a better offer. You'll decide to take it. I'll go on the record saying how indispensable you were and that you'll be greatly missed."

"I'm not talking about party politics and my career. I'm talking about us, you and me and how I feel." Kelly felt her face. She was surprised to feel real tears streaming down her cheeks. She was disgusted by her display of weakness.

"I'm so sorry, but we knew that this could not continue indefinitely." He reached for her, offering comfort.

Kelly pulled away.

"I'll make sure you get another job," he promised. "Until then, I'll continue to pay your salary. You don't have to worry about finances."

"Just stop. Please. Just stop." Kelly wiped away her tears and straightened her skirt. She wouldn't allow him the pleasure of feeling better. Kelly laughed. She buttoned her shirt and threw his speech on the desk. She went to her office and quickly tossed her belongings into a small box. She was surprised how few personal items she'd accumulated in her office after so much time at the White House.

As she left her office, she realized how much she'd miss working with Christopher. She didn't know when she'd fallen in love with him, but she knew it was an inconvenience that she would have to get over.

On her way home, Kelly called Senator Balile. He was not going to be pleased.

****

Marcus sipped a lukewarm cup of coffee as he sat outside the Campbells' home, waiting for Jennifer and Justin to emerge. After having watched the house for a few days, he knew that Pastor Campbell usually left for the church around 6:00 AM, and his wife usually left shortly thereafter to go to work at a small boutique in the city. He waited for the Campbells to leave. He wanted to avoid any more deaths than necessary. He hadn't expected the task to take such an emotional toll on him. Jennifer and her son were strangers, and he'd done far worse things to people he'd known, but somehow, this was different. He was different.

Marcus checked his watch again. It was already 9:30, and no one had emerged from the dwelling. Marcus became concerned that maybe he had missed them.

Suddenly, the door opened and a woman slowly emerged, holding the hand of a young boy. Marcus released a sigh of relief. He poured out the remainder of his coffee and wiped the condensation off of the window for a better view. Marcus squinted to identify his targets. Yes. It was definitely Justin.

He got out of his car and cautiously approached. He planned to follow them from a distance until he could make his move. As he got closer, he stopped dead in his tracks.

He was only partly correct. The boy was Justin, but the woman holding his hand was not Jennifer. It was Kira.

"What are you doing here?" Kira smiled as she recognized the man approaching them. "You startled me."

Marcus opened his mouth to make an excuse, but he could not speak.

"Are you okay?" Kira asked Marcus. She realized from the look on his face that something must be horribly wrong. She gave the young boy a gentle nudge. "Justin, go back inside."

"We have to talk," Marcus managed to mumble through trembling lips.

"Come inside."

Marcus followed Kira inside the house. She introduced him to Jennifer.

"And these are my parents." Kira motioned to Pastor Campbell and his wife. "We can go into the den for some privacy."

Marcus followed her toward the den but suddenly froze. He had come face to face with the moment that would decide the rest of his life, and the thought of making a mistake terrified him. "I think your parents and Mrs. Drake should join us."

"How did you know my last name?" Jennifer asked.

"I know a lot more about you than you know." Marcus handed Kira the picture of Jennifer and Justin with the Campbells' address imprinted on the back of the photo.

"Maybe Justin could wait in another room," Marcus suggested.

"You're frightening me." Kira searched his deep eyes and saw something she'd never seen there before—fear.

"I don't mean to frighten you. I wish there was another way. I'd give anything not to have to tell you this."

Jennifer sent Justin into the next room to watch television.

Marcus began by first explaining to them about what had happened to him all those years ago when he was first taken. He told them about the Triad and about his training. He told them about reporting to Neal each month and lastly, he told them about his orders. This last part he said quickly, as if he feared that he'd lose his nerve otherwise.

Kira grabbed for the phone. "We have to call the police."

Marcus stopped her. "You can't." She saw his knife and cried out in fear. "No, don't be frightened. I'm not going to harm any of you. If I were, I would not be telling you this. As far as the Triad is concerned, the second I broke my code of silence, I became one of you. I am and will forever be seen by them as an enemy to the cause. My decision is final. There is no going back."

"If you're not going to kill us, then why don't you want us to call the police?" Jennifer asked.

"Technology today has become so advanced that they can solve crimes from years ago, yet children have been abducted by this serial abductor for years without a single suspect. How do you think that is possible?"

"Are you suggesting that the police may be involved?"

"The Triad's power reaches all the way up to top members of our government. Everyone is a potential threat. I'm taking a risk just being here."

"What made you change your mind?" Pastor Campbell questioned.

"What do you mean?"

"You brought a knife, so I have to assume that you were going to go through with your orders. Something had to have changed your mind."

"You." Marcus turned to Kira. "I've feared the Triad my entire life. I've never allowed myself to disobey a single order. I've done horrible things in their name because blind obedience was the only way to survive. You can't understand; so many children came and went. Few survived more that a few weeks. Those of us who did survive did so by learning to obey without question."

"You weren't given a choice." Pastor Campbell's tone was almost apologetic. "No one blames you."

Marcus looked away. "Until now, my own survival was the most important thing to me. I mean, I wish I could say that I've seen the light and have turned from my wicked ways, but the truth is, now there is someone I care about more than my own safety. I love you, Kira. I never expected to care for you. At first, I just expected you to be my ticket into the inner circle, but now ... I don't expect you to forgive me. How could you not hate me?"

"Why would I hate you?" Kira stopped him. "You saved our lives at the expense of you own well-being."

"You were a child," Jennifer added. "In so many ways, you still are, but despite the real threat to your own personal safety, you are here, warning us. You say you're doing this so that you don't lose Kira, but you could have waited until she was gone. You said it yourself—the Triad's power is far reaching. Kira never would have known." Jennifer trembled at the thought of how close they'd come to a horrific death.

Kira looked to her father. "What do we do now?"

"First, we need to contact Aaron. His life may be in danger as well. Then we call an emergency FLOCK meeting." Pastor Campbell smiled reassuringly at Marcus. "Everything works according to his will for those who believe. Are you a believer, son?"

Marcus shook his head. Despite his parents' and Kira's prompting, he had resisted. He had not though it worth his consideration, but at that moment, he felt something inside him stir. It was a longing he had never felt before.

"Would you like the assurance of knowing that he who holds the world is supporting you?"

"Yes."

Pastor Campbell led Marcus in the prayer of salvation. They all took turns embracing him. Marcus called his parents, while Pastor Campbell called Aaron.

****

Balile waited in a limousine outside Kelly's apartment. As Kelly approached, she saw that he was not alone. The driver opened the door for Kelly, and at once she recognized the other passenger. She had not seen him since he'd taken her to New York years ago to meet Christopher. She instantly stepped away from the door.

"Please." The man stretched out his hand toward her. "Join us."

Kelly reluctantly climbed onto the seat beside the gentleman. She diverted her eyes toward the floor of the car as they made their way down familiar streets. She did not know where she was being taken, but she was sure that she would not pass this way again. She felt the man's eyes on her, and it struck fear at the very core of her being. She didn't fear her own mortality, but she did fear the way in which she was to meet that fate. The Triad was not known for its restraint or mercy.

Kelly summoned all her courage and tried to explain. "I did everything I could!"

"We are not rewarded for our good intentions; rather, we are rewarded and disciplined for our successes and our failures. Is this not the Triad way?" The man chastised.

"Yes."

"It is good that you at least remember that much, so there is no need to remind you what the punishment is for failing the Triad."

Kelly lowered her head in silence. She did not speak again.

The limousine pulled into a parking garage where Balile's car was waiting. As he exited the limo, he looked back at Kelly. She did not make a sound, but her eyes pleaded with him. He knew, just as she did, that there was nothing he could do for her. He saw a single tear race down her cheek as the door closed behind him, and the limo pulled out of sight. It was the last time he saw her.

****

Aaron called Christopher to alert him to the situation. After comparing notes, they suspected that there may have been a connection between the threat on Aaron's family and the anonymous photos of Christopher and Kelly.

"I don't believe in coincidences." Christopher lowered his voice to a whisper, as if he feared someone's hearing him. "You know that I've believed for a long time that Balile was dangerous. He has an obvious agenda that he intends to accomplish by any means necessary."

"We don't have any proof."

"Are you willing to wait? You can't convince me that he or someone he represents was not directly involved in President McIntyre's death, as well as the others. If we don't go on the offensive now, it may be too late."

"You're right, but what do you want to do?" Aaron asked.

"I don't know yet, but we have to do something. I say, first we protect our families. I'm going to increase security for Tracy and my daughter. I hope you'll allow me to assign someone to you and your family."

"I'd appreciate that. Until we know what's happening, we have to take precautions. I think the Campbell family and Marcus and his family would also benefit from additional security." Aaron was grateful for the additional security. Jennifer's and Justin's safety meant everything to him.

"Consider it done. What are your feelings concerning Marcus? He was gone for a long time. Can he be trusted?" Christopher asked.

"He didn't have to expose his connection to the Triad. No one suspected him, and Pastor Campbell feels he is credible."

"I guess you're right. He has nothing to gain from deceit," Christopher agreed.

"Do you really think this has something to do with my testimony?"

"Can you think of any other reason your family would be targeted."

"It just seems so unimaginable that anyone could perceive me as such a threat that they would be willing to harm my wife and child."

"You underestimate your influence."

"Why not just kill me?"

"Why kill you, when they can force you to support their agenda. If they had Justin, what couldn't they make you do?" Christopher understood the position his friend faced. "I'll understand if you decide not to testify. You have your family to consider."

"Are you giving up your position? If my family is in danger over this, I imagine so is yours."

"I can't change my position every time someone makes a threat, credible or not. I took an oath to do what is best for the American people, and I plan to uphold that promise."

"Well, I took an oath to do what is best for God's people. How can I teach my son to stand for Christ and trust in his divine protection if I run the first time I am challenged?" Aaron was convinced—now more than ever—that he had to testify. If the devil was this determined to keep the Congress from hearing what he had to say, then he knew that it was a message that he had to deliver. He trusted God to protect him and his family.

"I guess we're in this, then." Christopher was glad to have Aaron's support.

"I suppose so," Aaron agreed.

CHAPTER TWENTY-ONE

Eric arrived home early that Friday. Katelyn had been having some early labor pains, and he wanted to be with her. Talen had been born almost a month early, and Eric wondered if this delivery would be a repeat. Maybe Sharay was right. Maybe this child really was more than a Talen look-alike. Maybe he really was Talen.

"How are you feeling?" Eric rubbed Katelyn's back to soothe her. It had been the only thing that gave her any relief when she was pregnant with Talen.

"I feel much better. I'm so glad you're here."

"Where else would I be?"

Just as Eric leaned over to kiss her, they heard the dog barking. He looked outside to see what was upsetting him. The dog was standing over Talen, who had collapsed beside the swing.

Katelyn rushed to assist their son, while Eric called for an ambulance. Katelyn began performing CPR. She continued until the paramedics arrived. She and Eric followed in their car and arrived at the hospital just behind the ambulance. They hurried inside to be with their son. Suddenly, Katelyn felt a sharp pain that caused her to double over. A nurse quickly ran over to assist her. Eric was torn. He wanted to help his wife, but he needed to be with their son.

"Go," Katelyn insisted. "Take care of Talen."

Eric hurried to catch up with the doctors as they sped Talen to the ER. Eric looked back just in time to see them whisk Katelyn off to the delivery room. Eric watched helplessly through the glass as the doctors hurried about the room, fighting to save the young child's life ... but to no avail.

Eric was allowed into the room to say good-bye to his son.

One of the doctors attempted to explain. "I'm so sorry. We did all we could."

"I want an autopsy."

"But …"

"Is that a problem?"

"No."

"I want it performed right away, but not here. I do not want you to alert his doctor. Will that be a problem?"

"No. I can make the arrangements."

Eric could not explain why he needed an autopsy to confirm what should have been obvious. Everyone, including the emergency room staff, was aware of Talen's rare illness, but something Neal had said in their last conversation had struck a chord with Eric, and he couldn't shake it.

"I will let you know when they are ready to move the body," the doctor said.

"Thank you." Eric went to find his wife.

****

Neal hung up the phone. The only thing worse than getting bad news was having to deliver it. He knew that losing Marcus was bad enough, but failure to locate him was unacceptable. As Marcus' handler outside of the Center, he had worried that he might be blamed for Marcus' betrayal. Fortunately for Neal, however, that honor had fallen upon Marcus' trainer at the Center.

"What did they say?" Angela waited nervously to learn what was to be her husband's fate and, ultimately, her own.

"They said that my responsibility for Marcus is finished. They'll locate him and handle the situation on their end. My priority now is to the child. He is my only responsibility."

"Does Eric know this?"

"I will explain everything to my brother when I feel the time is right. He's already dealing with the loss of a child. That can't be easy, no matter how expected."

****

Eric sat listening to the minister's words of comfort at the graveside of their son. He lovingly stroked Katelyn's hand. He was glad that the minister's words were bringing her some small comfort, even if they were doing nothing for him. He felt the baby stir. He wished he could share the secret of the baby with her, but he knew that she would never understand.

Eric felt empty. Though he knew that Talen lived on in their son, Collier, it was not the same. He could not explain the way he felt. As a scientist, he understood that Collier and Talen were genetically the same child, but as a father, he knew better.

He glanced around at all the well-wishers who had come to pay their respects. Some he recognized from the hospital and around the neighborhood; many others he didn't know at all. Katelyn had explained that they were members of the church she and Talen had joined just before Talen had become sick. Although they had not been able to attend as often as they would have liked because of Talen's illness, they both had come to love the church and its members. She was not surprised that several of the members had taken time out of their busy day to show their support.

As the funeral drew to an end, a young woman sang a solo, and the minister made his way over to Eric and Katelyn to offer condolences. He invited them to call if he could be of any service.

"Thank you, Pastor. The service was lovely." Katelyn smiled bravely.

"It was my pleasure. I hope that you will continue to visit us as often as you are able."

"Yes. I would love that."

"Thank you very much." Eric shook the minister's hand. "We've invited everyone back to the house. I hope you will be able to come."

"Yes, of course."

As Eric escorted Katelyn to the car, he caught a glimpse of his brother in the crowd. "Go ahead. I'll be right along."

"Is anything wrong?" Katelyn was concerned. Though she knew that Eric would never admit it, she recognized how difficult this was for him. She understood that he felt that he had to be strong for her, but she wished he would allow her to comfort him as well.

"No, I just saw someone I thought would not be able to attend. I wanted to thank him and invite him to the house," he reassured her.

"I'll take Katelyn and the baby to the car," Sarah offered. "You go talk to Neal."

Eric was shocked. He had not been aware that Sarah had known that Neal had returned. He nodded and made his way over to where Neal was waiting.

"I wasn't expecting you," Eric said.

"We wanted to make sure you and the baby were doing all right."

"We? By 'we' are you referring to the Triad."

"Yes, among others, like Angela and Sharay. Remember them?"

"What do you want? Why are you really here?" Eric asked.

"What a remarkable child. I never got to meet my nephew, Talen. I hope you will allow me to get to know him now."

"I'm afraid you're too late. Talen is dead. My baby's name is Collier, not Talen. I would love for you to meet him, but only if we can come to an understanding that my life and the lives of my wife and child are our own. We are not pawns to be manipulated by the Triad."

"I see."

"Our last conversation really unnerved me."

"How so?" Neal asked.

"You made it seem as if my life and the lives of my family had been completely orchestrated by the Triad."

"Why is that such a bad thing? Look at how much they've done for you. If not for them, you would have lost Talen forever."

"They haven't done anything for us. Everything they've done has been for their prophesied holy family. We're not them."

"If you're so sure about that, then why do you care?"

"Maybe I'm wondering just how involved they've been in our lives."

"What's that suppose to mean?" Neal asked.

"Whose decision was it to fake your death? What about our parents' deaths? Why did Sarah rush to our aid? She barely knew us." Eric continued to fire one question after the other.

"She was friends with our parents. You know that."

"She knows that you are alive. Has she always known? Was she involved? She is Triad, after all."

"You already knew that, and no, I contacted her after Talen's death."

"When I told her that I thought I was in love with Sharay, it was she who said it was too soon for me to make a commitment. And when I called her from the lab that day, and told her that Sharay was pregnant, and that I thought that I had overreacted when she told me, Sarah was the one who encouraged me to insist on the abortion. I wanted to ask Sharay to marry me, but Sarah insisted that it was not the right time. She said rushing things could destroy our relationship. Were those her feelings—or the wishes of the Triad?"

"You're being paranoid," Neal insisted. "There's been no conspiracy."

"I've spoken to Sharay. Our meeting that day at the conference was staged. She admits that she was instructed to offer me back my job at Grayson Labs."

"Why don't you say what you are really trying to say?"

"I think it's ironic that both our parents died uncommon deaths. Maybe I'm wondering just how far the Triad is willing to go to orchestrate the future they want."

"As far as necessary."

"Why doesn't that frighten you?" Eric asked.

"I've learned to trust the wisdom of the Triad."

"Learned? Or were you brainwashed?"

Neal laughed.

"I'm serious. Who told you that our father was a threat to me? How did you even know to go to the hotel? Did you decide on your own that he was trying to harm me, or did they convince you of that?"

Neal became angry. "I did what I had to do to protect you."

"That's right, from the Christian fanatics. The same crazy people who comforted me after your death and who are comforting my wife right now."

"Don't forget who gave you back Talen."

"You preserved his DNA, but no one can return my son to me. I've had to accept that, but you know, I was wondering about something."

"You seem to have everything figured out. I can't imagine what."

"The Triad was in bed with Sharay before I lost my job. Why?"

"What are you suggesting?"

"I had a private autopsy performed," Eric explained. "Talen's results suggest that despite having all the symptoms of his diagnosed ailment, his organs showed no signs of the disease that was supposed to have killed him."

"What does that mean?"

"It means that my son died from something other than the illness I spent his final days trying to cure."

"Have you told any one else about you suspicions?"

"What would I tell them? Should I tell them about the phantom group that helped me and my ex-lover to impregnate my wife with the clone of our recently murdered child?"

"Talen was not murdered," Neal insisted.

"I wish I could believe that. I hate thinking that I've been in bed with the very people who systematically are destroying my entire family—my mother, my father, my in-laws, and now my son."

"You're wrong."

"I wish I could share your faith, but either way, I want them to stay away from my family, because at best they are obsessive, and at worst they are dangerous. I plan to speak to Sarah later; but if you and she want to stay in our lives, you're going to have to cut your ties to the Triad. I don't want them anywhere near me or mine ever again, or I will go to the police."

Neal watched as Eric walked toward the car where Sarah and Katelyn were waiting. He called Balile immediately. "We have a problem."

Chapter Twenty-Two

"Hello. You've reached the Clayton County emergency hotline. Due to unusually heavy calling, all of our dispatchers are handling other calls. If this is an emergency, please hold the line, and your call will be—"

"Hello, Clayton County emergency hotline. This is Susan. How may I help you?"

"My baby is missing! Someone has taken my baby! Help us, please! You have to help us!" Katelyn tried to remain calm, but she could feel herself losing control, as her heart began to race and her breath came more quickly.

"Please, try to follow me. You have to stay calm. I want to help you, but first you must help me. Can you tell me where you are?" Susan realized that the woman on the phone was on the verge of hysterics.

"Home." Her voice was barely more than a desperate breath of air.

"What can you tell me about your baby?" Susan tried to obtain as much information as possible.

Katelyn tried but was unable to answer. She closed her eyes tightly to slow the flood of tears that threatened to overwhelm her. Finally, she found the strength to speak, but all she was able to tell the dispatcher was that her baby was gone.

"Do you know who has taken your baby? I know this is hard, but I need you to try to focus." Susan continued to try to calm the woman, but the only audible sounds that came from her were sobs. "Are you sure your baby is gone?"

Suddenly, Susan heard another voice come through the phone. "Who is there with you?" she asked. "Please let me speak to whoever is there with you." She heard muffled conversation and then another voice on the line—a man's voice.

"Hello, we live at 32 Crescent Place! Please send someone! My son has been taken!" His voice was shaky but intelligible, and for that, Susan was grateful.

****

Sarah didn't know how long it would be before her car was discovered, so she parked her car near the subway. She hoped to buy herself as much time as possible by misdirecting the authorities. As Sarah hurried down the street toward her secret rendezvous, she clutched the small bundle as if it were precious gold.

Sarah hid around the corner from the small diner and waited for the signal. She waited for what seemed like an hour before she saw it. The headlights of a small car blinked once and then again. She waited a moment more. There it was—the third blink. She handed her small cargo to the man behind the wheel as she climbed into the car.

"I waited a long time for you. I expected you to be here when we arrived." Sarah could not hide her annoyance. She'd been terrified ever since she'd left Eric and Katelyn's home with Collier.

"I've been here half the night. I spotted you the second you arrived. I just needed to wait to ensure that the coast was clear before attempting contact," Neal explained.

"What are our orders?"

"We are to fly to Rome to the head offices of the Triad. We have reservations for tonight. The sooner we're in the air, the safer we'll both feel."

Neal made his way to the airport as quickly as he could without drawing unwanted attention. As they boarded the plane with the fake passports provided to them by the Triad, Neal's thoughts turned to his brother. He couldn't imagine the pain his actions were going to cause him so soon after the lost of his only child. He'd have given anything for there to have been another way.

****

It was morning when the officers had finished collecting evidence. Eric and Katelyn had been up all night answering questions, but there were more questions than there were answers.

"How can you be sure that Sarah wasn't involved?" The officer pressed.

"She loves our son. She'd never do anything to harm him or us. She didn't have a reason to take him," Katelyn insisted. "I'm frightened for her. The kidnappers must have taken her as well."

"Why would they take her and not you?"

"Maybe she caught them."

"Or maybe she helped them." The officer's instincts warned him that this was an inside job. "There were no signs of forced entry, and you and your husband both said you felt as though you'd been drugged. Was there any one else here who could have drugged you?"

"We had just buried our son. Our house was full of people, but I can't imagine that any of them would wish us harm."

"Sir, you haven't said much. Is there anything you can add that might help?"

"No," Eric lied. He suspected Sarah the moment he realized that she was missing. Since learning that she was a member of the Triad, he had begun to question everything she'd ever said or done. His entire life had been a lie, and he didn't know whom to trust.

"Your wife told me that this Sarah raised you and your brother."

"She took us in after our parents died."

"Can you think of anyone else who might intend harm to you and your family?" the officer asked. "Did anyone seem at all suspicious at your son's funeral? Was there anyone you didn't recognize?"

"My wife is a leading pediatric surgeon, and she attends a very large church. I hardly recognized anyone, but no one seemed suspicious."

"What about that man at the gravesite?" Katelyn suddenly remembered Neal's appearance at the cemetery. "You looked surprised to see him."

"He was just an old colleague of mine. I wasn't expecting him to see him."

"Fine." The officer put way his notebook. "Let us know if you think of anything. Your wife gave us a list of everyone she remembered seeing here yesterday. We'll be in contact after we've had an opportunity to follow up."

"Thank you." Eric escorted the officer to the door.

"What are we going to do?" Katelyn turned to Eric.

"I need to make a call." Eric went into the den for privacy. He tried Neal's number, but there was no answer. He sat staring at the phone, trying to decide what to do next. He picked up the phone and began to dial the number of the only person he felt could help them.

****

Aaron hung up the phone.

"Who was that?" Jennifer called from the kitchen. She grabbed a soda before retuning to the den.

"Chris," Aaron answered. "The House and Senate votes were both close, but they went our way."

"It's amazing that it happened so soon, but I never doubted, and I'm sure your testimony played no small part. I'm just happy this is over. Maybe we can stop looking over our shoulder." Jennifer joined Aaron on the couch.

"Not yet, but soon. I'm sure the church will be happy just to get rid of all the increased security."

"I don't know—they seemed pretty proud of you for taking a stand. Even Mrs. Maple seemed less annoyed than usual."

"She does seem to be coming around."

"When the president holds you up as a shining example of heroism, it carries a little weight. Besides, I think she realizes that you're for real and not just looking to make a name for yourself. You put your life on the line for righteousness."

"We all did," Aaron insisted.

"I was a little worried when the church's anniversary had to be postponed, but all is well that ends well."

"I'm just happy that the anniversary went off without any unwanted attention." Aaron agreed.

"I think everyone was relieved."

The phone rang as they settled in for the evening.

"Let me guess who that is." Jennifer teased.

Aaron's smile faded as he listened to the caller. They agreed to meet.

"Who was that?" Jennifer asked.

"Eric."

****

"I was surprised to hear from you after all these years." Pastor Campbell could tell that Eric had not slept, and the minister was concerned for his friend's health.

"Thank you for agreeing to meet with me," Eric said. "Were you able to contact Christopher?"

"Yes."

"Did he agree to meet with me?"

"Yes. There is more going on than even you know. He will meet us when he is able, but there is someone else here to see you."

Eric turned to see Aaron standing in the doorway. It was as if all the years apart had never existed. Eric told him about Sharay, and the baby, and about the Triad, and of his suspicions concerning the Triad's involvement in Collier's abduction.

From all that Eric shared, Aaron and Pastor Campbell began to wonder if they were the same group that Marcus had described. They took Eric to meet with Marcus. The FLOCK had placed him in a safe house under their protection.

It did not take long for Eric and Marcus to determine that they were speaking about the same group. As soon as Marcus described Neal, Eric was sure that it had been his brother who had ordered the death of Aaron's wife.

"Do you know why they want your son?" Marcus asked.

"They believe he is the fulfillment of some sort of prophesy."

"I don't see how that is possible. Their prophesy clearly states that the child will be born without parents, and he will be the incarnation of their lord."

"Every child has to have parents. How do they expect to fulfill such an absurd prophesy?" Aaron protested.

Suddenly, Eric understood. "Not every child."

"What? How is that possible?"

"Your Jesus was supposed to have had a surrogate mother and no father, right? It's supposed to be what allowed him to fulfill his destiny as the Messiah. He used a loophole to cheat the system by being born like a man but without the sin of mankind."

They were surprised at how much Eric knew about the Bible.

"Well, as far as the Triad is concerned, my son doesn't have parents either—at least, not like you and I have parents." Reluctantly, Eric told them about Collier's creation. "That was why they supported our research. They never intended for Talen to get well. They just needed his DNA and our research."

"I know that you are not a believer," said Pastor Campbell, "but I hope you will allow us to pray for you and your family. There is obviously more at work here than the natural."

"I don't know that I am ready to accept that, but I'll accept your prayers. Thank you."

Pastor Campbell led the men in a prayer, asking for God's protection and mercy for all of their families.

CONCLUSION

Balile met Neal at the airport and escorted them to the Center to meet with the board. Neal felt anxious; he could not help but remember his last trip to the Center. He tried to push his fears out of his mind. He recognized that this was going to be the most important thing to happen to him in his life. He was not going to allow his fears to cause him to make a fatal mistake.

As the car pulled up to the Center, Neal held onto Collier. It wasn't until he exited the car that he fully grasped the scope of the situation. Neal was taken aback to see thousands of people surrounding the car. As surprised as he was to see so many people waiting for them, he was even more astonished by the absolute silence. It was so quiet, he could have heard a feather drop.

Neal turned in time to see a woman approaching, her head slightly bowed. It wasn't until she raised her head to look upon the child that he recognized her as the board director he'd had the misfortune to insult on his last visit to the Center.

"Welcome home, my lord." She knelt in front of Neal. Suddenly, in unison, the entire crowd knelt. It was then that he realized that they were all there to see the child.

The woman led Neal and Sarah into the Center, where the rest of the board was waiting.

The senior member of the board approached. He gently stroked Collier's forehead before turning his attention to Neal. "You have accomplished what has been foretold in our prophesy for thousands of years."

Neal didn't know what to say.

"It has been decided that you should raise our lord, and that Sharay should be his mother." The man spoke for the others.

"You must mean her sister—my wife, Angela," Neal insisted.

"No, we mean Sharay. Angela has served her purpose. If you wish to keep her around, that is not a problem, as long as it is okay with Sharay."

Neal wasn't sure how Angela and Sharay were going to take this news, but he suspected that they were not being given a choice.

"Don't worry." The man reassured Neal. "We will handle everything. Angela may resist a little at first, but we can be quite persuasive when necessary. I know that we can continue to depend on you."

"Yes, of course you can." Neal steadied himself. He felt the baby's warmth and knew that the child approved. "I am willing to do anything for our lord. It is my pleasure to serve."

"We all must be willing to lose our lives if we are to save our souls," the man proclaimed.

"Amen," they all echoed.

"The sacrifices made by your family have not gone unnoticed."

Printed in the United States
145032LV00002B/84/P

9 780595 480975